Lock Down Publications and Ca$h
Presents

RELENTLESS

GOON 2

HARDCORE & GRIMY

Written By
PRINCE A. TAUHID

First Edition 2025

Printed in the United States of America

This is a work of fiction. Names, characters, places, and incidents either are products of the author's imagination or are used fictitiously. Any similarity to actual events or locales or persons, living or dead, is entirely coincidental.

Lock Down Publications
P.O. Box 944
Stockbridge, GA 30281
www.lockdownpublications.com

Like our page on Facebook: Lock Down Publications
www.facebook.com/lockdownpublications.ldp

Stay Connected with Us!

Text **LOCKDOWN** to 22828 to stay up-to-date with new releases, sneak peaks, contests and more…

Like our page on Facebook:
Lock Down Publications

Join Lock Down Publications/The New Era Reading Group

Visit our website:
www.lockdownpublications.com

Follow us on Instagram:
Lock Down Publications

Email Us: We want to hear from you!

PROLOGUE

2019...

Tap-Tap-Tap!

There was a knock on the front door to the home of an elderly woman. She was the mother of Melvin "Parlay" Anderson. Her name was Mrs. Irene Anderson. The man who appeared at her doorstep was unknown to her. This was his first time in the neighborhood actually.

"Who's there?" Mrs. Irene let out from the kitchen. She made steps in the direction at this point.

"I'm a representative of National Insurance Company, ma'am," stated the gentleman. "May I please speak with you briefly?" he requested.

The old lady opened the door and initiated the talk through the burglar bars that separated the two. "May I help you with something, sir?" she asked.

"Yes, ma'am. How are you? I'm Edward Godfrey from National Insurance. And if possible, I'd like to offer you the opportunity to be provided one of our special health care policies, that specifically coincides with the Affordable Care Act that's best known as *Obamacare*. The current president, Donald Trump, is seriously trying to undermine everything *Obamacare* provides. And this is especially so, regarding the benefits that our great senior citizens like yourself enjoy. There's no way we can allow for this to happen," the representative stated. He spoke in a convincing and persuasive tone.

"This darn president we have now is really doing *us* an injustice, ain't he? Definitely so to *us* Black folks! Is it okay for me to speak this way with you?" Mrs. Irene said, attempting to know whether or not she had the leeway to speak candidly to the fellow who sought to enter her home and sell her health insurance.

"Yes, ma'am. It's perfectly okay. You're absolutely fine by honestly expressing yourself. And if I may, could I please come inside to go over a few things I've got to offer?" he asked.

Mrs. Irene appeared hesitant to respond quickly. She stared the guy directly in the eyes as to somewhat gauge his energy and possible overall intent. She aimed to get a feel for if or not the outward appearance and presentation, matched what he may have had hidden within. Following the prolonged engagement, she finally obliged and welcomed the well-dressed guy in a suit into her home. "Yes. Please, sir. Come in."

As the man, who Mrs. Irene had never seen before, entered through the doorway, he extended his hand and stated a name once more. "Edward Godfrey is my name, ma'am, if you missed it the first time," he reiterated. She accepted the handshake and then gestured with her free hand for him to have a seat. The guest chair was closest to the door. It still remained open with the bars unlocked.

The slightly tall man brought along a brown leather tote bag that contained a laptop amongst other things. He had knowledge that the old lady would be home all by her lonely at the particular hour of the day. There wasn't anything to worry about regarding someone appearing to interrupt the special occasion he had in stow.

The son, Melvin, was away in the north, New York City. There was urgent business there that needed his attention. Also, Ms. Sheila, the helpful neighbor, always worked from 8 A.M. to 4 P.M. throughout the weekday at the local Walgreens drug store. She wouldn't be around to witness or hear anything either on the Tuesday morning that was upon them. It was an unfortunate situation taking shape against Mrs. Irene, being that the intended target was the son, Melvin, himself. But, he seemed a difficult type of creature to corner and have the drop placed upon. Dude was hard to pinpoint. Therefore, word was ordered that his mother was to be the one to get it now, instead of him. The sins of the son would be bore on the mother.

The person who Melvin had run afoul with, was determined to teach him a valuable lesson in manners. Something to take heed of moving forward was that he shouldn't fuck with the wrong man ever again, and shouldn't try to turn a man's daughter against him. Atop this, he definitely wanted Melvin to make note to not ever take sides with the enemy against him, a man who could make life a living hell if he so pleased. There was a lot at stake.

"So, young man," Mrs. Irene continued, "please make me aware of what improved policy plans you have to offer that's better than the one I already own with the company I'm with," she stated.

"It's right here, ma'am," he responded and slowly made a motion like he was going into the tote bag to retrieve something. "It's all right here."

Suddenly, the man lunged forward and gripped the old lady around the throat with his powerful hands. She was overtaken with ease. He made a maneuver and was now behind her. One hand was placed over her mouth to muffle any screams, and his other arm was situated around her waist to drag her to the back bedroom. With what little strength she did have, there was an attempt to squirm and twist to get loose. This was to no avail. The elderly lady was no match for the hired assassin. He slapped her around ruthlessly and without mercy. There wasn't a care in the world that she was a seventy-something year old woman. He had orders to do what he had to do, and there were no exceptions to the rule.

The attacker pulled out a pair of shoelaces from his pocket and pushed the woman onto the bed. He began to tie her hands behind her back and her feet at the ankles. She was now a hostage.

"Lord, no! Please! No, young man! In God's name, what are you doing?" Mrs. Irene shouted with the strongest breath of wind she could muster up.

"Shut the fuck up, bitch!" the intruder retorted, following up with a volley of vicious slaps to her face.

Whop . . . whop . . . whop . . . whop!

The guy lifted the frail woman from the bed then slammed her hard onto the floor. "Where is that fucking son of yours, Melvin!?" he asked in an aggressive manner.

In a whimper, she offered a reply. "I have no idea, young man. Not at all. What is this about anyway?" The agony and pain from the physical assault was setting in.

"Your no-good son, done really fucked up this time, Misses! He really has. Since we can't quite seem to catch up with him, it all now falls on you. Your son dragged you into his bullshit, Miss Lady. I'm sorry it has to be like this. But, it is what it is," the guy declared.

"How about you call him and see what the two of you can work out?" Mrs. Irene suggested

"What's his phone number?!"

"I got it written inside the back cover of the phone book in the kitchen."

"Don't you make a fuckin' sound while I go get it, you hear me?!" he stated while mean mugging her and pointing a finger in her face.

No sooner than he made a turn to go toward the kitchen, Mrs. Irene began to vehemently yell for help. "Somebody help me, please! Help! In Jesus name, someone help me in here!" Her cries for help went unheard.

The hired goon picked up the pace in his actions and rummaged through the phone and address books for Melvin's number and possibly other information he could use. He clutched the journals then ran back to the bedroom to silence Mrs. Irene for her disobedience to his command.

"Didn't I tell you to keep quiet and not say shit, you dumb old bitch?!" he shouted and then spit in her face prior to taking things a step further and punching her in the nose, knocking her out on impact. He then straddled her and began to viciously squeeze hard on her throat. He stayed in this position until her windpipe caved in. He pressed harder and harder until the chest of the elderly lady stopped heaving. She was no more. He'd murdered her.

For the entire time while inside, the assailant was careful not to touch anything. There wasn't a need to perform a wipe down of the place. He simply stood to his feet, stepped back to the living room, strapped the tote bag with the laptop back across his shoulder, tucked the two books under an arm, and politely walked out of the house, closing the door behind him. He entered his car once more and drove away, unnoticed by anyone. This was a smooth criminal who had an appetite for murder.

PART ONE

Chapter 1

The Tale of the Tape . . .

The hitter that took out Melvin's mother, was ordered to do so by his uncle, leader, and boss, Mitchell Duvalier-Collins, aka "Long-Money Mitch." Mitch was a man who Melvin, aka "Parlay," had previously worked for at a club he co-owned. This was of course before everything went awry, leaving Melvin to pick and choose sides as he had. For Mitch, he had a personal score to settle with Melvin, being that he'd aligned himself in the ranks of a former friend/business partner but now an avowed enemy, Raymond Eugene Stephens. The two went separate ways and became bitter foes when Mr. Raymond made a business decision to sell the club they owned without Mitch's consent. Although there was much profit to be gained by the transaction, Mitch felt Mr. Raymond operated in an underhanded way as he had no intentions to sell. At any cost.

What prompted Mr. Raymond to make an exit from the nightlife business was that, he pursued a career in municipal politics. He held ambition and aspiration to be elected as mayor of Miami, and the strip club—amongst other things—would have tarnished the polished image he was looking to perpetuate to the voters he was looking to gain. Also, Mr. Raymond only sought to pay Mitch the principal in finances he'd originally invested and none of the profit which the business brought in through the years. Opposite of this, the *two were heavily tied together in the drug trade. They'd been so for decades. Rivals, competitors, and violators, had all been lined up and executed, all in the name of the bond they had, the business they'd conducted, and the brotherhood they'd established. Mr. Raymond saw to it that Mitch be cut from the narcotics supply line they maintained with the Mexican cartel they dealt with. This forced Mitch to scramble and seek out a new connect.*

War broke out with both sides suffering casualties. Melvin wound up being caught in the middle. A nephew of Mitch's, was eventually killed. The offense that the guy committed was that he attempted to rob and whack Melvin as he secretly laid up with the daughter of Mitch, Tisha. The two maintained a passionate love affair, although contested from those close to her. Mitch had an unrelenting issue with the fact that his daughter was involved with Melvin. However, he never had the opportunity to catch them together to do what he could to put an end to things. Also, Melvin now pledged his loyalty to Mr. Raymond, the most hated and despised enemy of Mitch.

As the drama edged on, both camps were completely oblivious to the real problems that they'd encountered long before they began to exchange blows. A federal mole was planted and had successfully penetrated the enterprise while the two men were on good terms. The special agent was able to gather critical and overwhelming evidence that held the potential to put the two powerful street lords away in prison for the remainder of their lives or worse, see to it that the death penalty be prescribed, due to the high volume of murders that were committed either by the two or upon their orders. They had not the slightest sense of awareness that they'd been infiltrated. The presumption was that their enterprise was airtight and that if any investigation was to ever be launched by the government, they would immediately know. A federal agent was on payroll by Mr. Raymond.

Meanwhile, Melvin united with his cousin, Vick, once more. He was a notorious gun trafficker and held a prominent position amongst a professional group of other weapons traffickers. This so happened to be the same occupation that Melvin had prior to his arrest and incarceration for seventeen years. Vick, on the other hand, had never been knocked and continued to gain riches by his sophisticated manipulation of the lax gun laws of the south and route up the "Iron Pipeline" to northern states to cash in with his material.

There was a new and improved way of doing things, and Vick was sure to thoroughly inform his cousin, Melvin, on everything that related to how he and his crew now conducted business. Vick's infantry of workers were a unique core of individuals.

Melvin, who primarily preferred to be called upon as Parlay, was again completely caught up in the activities of the underworld and had long lost sight and interest of doing any and all possible to stay free. The objective was to start up a legitimate business with his longtime girlfriend, Traci. But all this changed rather quickly once freed.

The animosity . . . the tension . . . and the beef . . . intensified and got far uglier in severity by the day. The battle fields were on many fronts. Each held ties to the grander schemes of things in one way, shape, form, or fashion. Implosion was always of imminent threat. Not to mention, bodies had already dropped, and would continue to do so. Blood was shed with more to be drawn. And this left only the most vicious and the most instinctive ones of relentless quality being those who were subject to survive the onslaught of wrath and eventually be able to avoid unfortunate demises that loomed. The saga dredged onward.

Chapter 2

Months Prior To . . .

Parlay made his way to his mother's house immediately after he'd taken aim and let off shots at the guy who was once a friend but then turned snitch, Calvin Prescott. This was a man who he long wished was served with a lethal dose of karma for testifying and helping put him away in prison. He was the person who ratted him out to the feds. Parlay had long desired to punish Calvin for both, the old and the new, behind having everything to do with him going to prison, and for having the gall and audacity to think that he could go on about life as peacefully as could be and not have to suffer any form of consequences for having a stain as a snitch on his resume.

When Parlay entered the house, he went straight to the bathroom. He then began to count out the shell casings from the gun. He'd fixed it to where the casings had spit from the gun and into the plastic bag he'd wrapped around his hand. They were stuck in place. He plucked them one by one.

"One . . . two . . . three . . . four . . . ." he whispered. "Eleven." *Damn! I let off that many shots at that clown ass nigga! What the fuck!* he thought.

The P89 Ruger pistol was withdrawn from his pants pocket. He removed the clip and ejected the round from the chamber. There was a need to get an accurate count to know that no amount of evidence was left behind.

13

"One . . . two . . . three . . . four . . . ." The whispering proceeded. There were a total of seven live rounds that remained out of eighteen, which meant, they all were accounted for. None got away. A huge amount of weight and worry was lifted from his consciousness. He was so relieved, as he had on no gloves when he'd began shooting. But now, the factor of fear was eliminated.

From that point, he took three casing at a time, wrapped them in a swath of tissue, and began to flush each toilet paper ball down the toilet. He'd performed this at least five times so to be assured that everything was thoroughly disposed of. No chances could be taken. It didn't matter that Calvin had no knowledge as to who tried to assassinate him. This was if he was lucky to have survived the attack. Parlay didn't know just yet.

He took a peep through the crevasse of the door and the frame of his mother's bedroom to check on her. She was still sound asleep. He wondered to himself how all of the flushing that had been done didn't manage to wake her. But the medication she was on, had her down and out cold. He darted to his room and began to get between his thoughts to process and take it all in. The firearm was broken down into separate pieces—the top portion from the bottom and all other components from those. He then took a t-shirt and ripped it into three parts. The gun fragments were wrapped and situated into small trash bags. The intent was to throw them out into a dumpster in three different locales. Of course, it would be at a later part of the night, once he left out again.

The TV was turned on and put on the news channel. The time was 11:00 P.M. He placed his phone on Airplane Mode so to not to be disturbed and have the opportunity to lay back to relax.

Chapter 3

Meanwhile...

Back at the house of Calvin Prescott's mother, the site of the shooting where Melvin took aim to kill him . . . the blasts of gunshots had awakened a number of people in the neighborhood. They looked out of windows, stuck their heads from the doorway inside, and did all else people do when trying to identify exactly where in the hell had all the shooting come from. Most importantly, had anybody been shot in the process?

As Calvin remained slumped to the floor inside the car, bleeding out heavily from his wounds, he began to think up what next to do to save his own life. He was delirious and light-headed. He slowly squirmed around on the interior of the car, seeking to locate his cell phone. It was recovered. The device was on the floor of the passenger side, next to the bag of food he had for himself and his family who awaited him in the house. Calvin was hit four times in the ambush and needed medical attention right away.

He hit the phone app icon to pull up the recent call log. He scrolled down to his mother's number and tapped it.

"Hello!" she answered.

"Mom," Calvin wheezed out into the phone.

"What, boy?! And where you at with that damn food anyway? We hungry over here. And somebody done did a whole lot of shooting out that door too. So, hurry and get here," she stated.

"Momma, help me. I'm hit. It was me who got shot," he revealed.

"What?! Lawd, no, son! Where you at?!" she shouted into the phone, now worried about her dear boy.

"I'm in the car out front the house."

"I'm on the way, son! Be easy. Momma on the way. Hold on. I'm coming," the mother declared. "Dave! Joe!" She called out for her boyfriend and her brother, who was also in the house. "Y'all come on. Calvin just got shot! I got him on the phone now. He's out there in the car," she stated to the men. The three of them rushed out the door to help Calvin.

The mother reached the car first, went around to the driver side door, opened and entered. "Calvin! Son! Where was you shot at, son?" she asked, apparently in a fit of hysterics.

"I don't know right off. I may be hit pretty badly though. I don't know how many times either. *Ahhh!* I feel these hot ass bullets burning though," he managed to hiss out.

"Well, don't continue to talk too much, son. Just try to keep calm."

"Okay. But could y'all please get me to the hospital?" Calvin pleaded.

"We will, son. I'm 'bout to call nine-one-one for the police and an ambulance right now," she let out. The cordless phone was still in her hand.

"No, Mom. Please. Y'all just drive me to the hospital, will you?" he demanded.

It was obvious that the mother was near panic mode and unable to properly think. She gave help to Calvin as he mustered up the strength necessary to maneuver his body from the driver seat, out the car, and into the vehicle once more on the backseat. He lay across with his legs bent at the knees and feet flat, awaiting to be driven to the nearest hospital. The mother spoke more.

"Okay, son. There you go. We got you situated, and we now on our way." She comforted him with her words while getting into the passenger seat. The brother of hers, Joe, would do the driving. "Here, Dave, get this phone. I'll call you later," she said lastly to the boyfriend. They then pulled off, enroute to get Calvin the medical attention he needed.

There was an elderly lady across the street from the home of Calvin's mother. She'd been scared shitless behind all the shooting that took place on the street she lived, prompting her to call the police. They'd finally arrived at her house. A conversation occurred between the three, the woman and the two officers who appeared. Calvin, the injured victim, was long gone by this time. The policemen made a quick canvass of the immediate area along the block, only to discover nothing that would indicate a shooting happened or even shots were fired. This made their explanation far easier for the convincing of the frightened civilian.

"Ma'am, we appreciate you making the call to report a potential crime. But there wasn't anything that we noticed which would signify or suggest a firearm was discharged. It probably was just a few young people out and about lighting fireworks or something like that. They're known for this type of thing," the elder of the two cops declared. They both were white.

"Okay, Officer. I didn't know what was going on. All I heard was a bunch of popping out this door. And, on instinct, I knew to contact you people. That's what my tax dollars give me the leeway to do. You're right though. It could have been a round of fireworks for all I know. No matter what, us old folks can't afford to take any chances," stated Mrs. Emma Jean Watkins.

"Well, ma'am, you have a nice night, okay? Everything is safe. Nothing wrong over here," said the burly second cop. He and the partner immediately made steps back to their patrol car to depart the premises.

Chapter 4

Parlay became restless and wasn't able to keep situated at his mother's home as previously anticipated. Also, he powered his phone back to active once again and was alerted through text messages that Traci had attempted to contact him. She was concerned. He'd been away from her house for far longer than she was told by him he would be. Not to mention the fact that he had his phone off during the time she made her calls. There were already enough complications going on in their relationship that involved suspicions of him cheating. And he didn't need any more gas to be thrown on the fire of hell he was already dwelling in. So, he got to his feet and exited the house and headed back to Traci's place.

While on the way, he dumped the gun parts in different locations as he intended to do. When he made it to his girlfriend's house, he took a quick shower and lay down to rest for the night. Traci did the same, now assured he was in her bed next to her and not that of some other female he may have had dealings with.

Parlay awakened the following morning in time to catch the six o'clock news. He was eager to know what the results of his shooting were. Did he get Calvin or not? Did he die? Was he near dead? What? The coverage detailing all he awaited to know finally revealed:

"A shooting that occurred near the intersection of Twenty-second Avenue and Seventy-fourth Street at about ten forty-one P.M. left one person critically wounded but in stable condition at Jackson Memorial Hospital. The early forties victim by the name of Calvin Prescott, was shot four times by an assailant's gun, as he returned home following a hunger run to the nearby Popeye's Chicken. He suffered a bullet inflicted to the upper left chest area, one to the left shoulder, the left portion of the abdomen, and a bullet to the left leg in the knee and shin. Mister Prescott reported to the police that someone pulled a drive-by shooting on him and that he didn't have a chance to get a look at the car that was driven or at the person who tried to end his life. Following the police investigators taking photographs of the vehicle Mister Prescott was assaulted in and eventually utilized to get him to the hospital, it was discovered that multiple rounds had been fired in his direction. The driver's side of the car was riddled with bullets. Officers did report to what is now known as the site of the incident—in front of the home of Mister Prescott's mother—to perform a search for possible spent shell casings or other evidence but turned up empty-handed in the process. Mister Prescott's words to the police and his official report was as follows:

'Whoever it was that shot me, you missed on my life. It just wasn't my time to die.'

"This is Joan Emerson from the newsroom reporting on the crime."

Parlay couldn't believe what he'd just heard. He was livid. *Fuck! Fuck-fuck-fuck! I didn't kill that piece of shit!* He vented like a madman in his own mind as he fumed inside. He stomped his feet to the floor as he sat on the couch in the living room. He bit down on his bottom lip, and he banged a fist on the coffee table. His tantrum caused Traci to step to the living room from her bedroom where she was getting dressed for work.

"Damn, baby! What seems to be wrong with you?!" she asked. There was a worried look about her face.

"Nothing! Ain't nothing wrong with me. I'm good!" He told a bold-faced lie. The look of anger about his face held the potential to intimidate the most elite unit of the Navy Seals had he wanted to. "Not a damn thing is wrong with me!"

Parlay then made his way to the bathroom to relieve himself of the coffee he'd drank in the last thirty minutes. Traci held her mouth wide and looked on at him in astonishment, as he passed her. She was also taken aback by the way he'd spoken to her and the tone of voice utilized. Parlay's thoughts ran wild in the moment.

The next chance I get, I gotta be sure to do better and kill that fuck-boy! He's definitely got to go! No doubt about it. And I gotta continue to lay low and not allow that pussy-ass nigga the opportunity to see me out and about around town. But he's dead as a motherfucka though! Dead as dead can be!

Chapter 5

In The Meantime . . .

Shortly before the day Parlay took aim at Calvin, another beef was playing out. One between Mr. Raymond and ex friend/business partner, Mitch. The nephew of Mitch—Roland—and his cohorts that assisted him—made it to the designated safe house that they were to report to with their kidnapped victim in tow. It was Jerome Maxwell aka "Big Mix." They had him handcuffed and chained to the floor. A set of ringed hooks had been locked on a cemented block to serve this purpose. The truck Big Mix was taken from was dismantled and the parts sold from it once the narcotics he was transporting was discovered and taken away by his abductors.

Roland had a few remarks for their hostage. "Well, damn, nigga! Had I known you were holding that much dope like we took from you, I would've been kidnapped and robbed you. Mark ass nigga!" He had on a ski mask to keep his face concealed. Roland then took it upon himself to bitch slap Big Mix with a hard backhand, all because he could.

Whop!

He spit on his head as well. "You had a lot of product you were moving. I need to know who the fuck it is you work for, nigga?" Roland demanded a response. The tape was snatched from Mix's mouth, ripping a patch of hair from his beard and mustache in the process.

"Go to hell, motherfucka! That's what you do," Mix muttered in a weak voice.

"Say what?!" Roland shot back.

"You heard what I said, nigga. Go-to-hell," Big Mix repeated.

"Okay, since you wanna play tough guy, I got a trick for that ass. Yeah, buddy. I got something for that ass. I tell you. And just so you'll know, we got all those pills you had and the money. We then destroyed that piece of shit truck of yours too."

At the point of Roland and the boys going through the vehicle in a thorough search for contraband, money, and other valuable possessions, the 400,000 pills Big Mix had picked up from the elder business partner of Mr. Raymond, one named Emanuel, the material that was to be delivered to an out of state customer, was discovered. The tracking device utilized to keep up with Big Mix was recovered from the truck prior to it being dismantled.

"If only you niggaz had any idea who y'all done fucked up and robbed. I promise you, the man who I work for, gonna put a ticket so large on you niggaz' heads, that the president, Donald Trump, may be tempted to take it up and send the military to get you bastards. Me and Mr. Raymond gonna have y'all niggaz' asses. You wait and see," Big Mix defiantly proclaimed.

"Nigga, shut the fuck up!" Roland retorted. He then kicked Big Mix in the mouth, claiming six of his teeth and badly damaging his lips.

Dazed beyond comprehension but still conscious to fight back with words, he threatened Roland once more. "You dead, motherfucka! Just know that much. You dead!"

"Yeah, yeah! Whatever. And I almost forgot to let you know. That so-called low-key spot you got in Miramar. I sent one of my guys to go raid the place, since you were nice enough to give us the key to it," Roland taunted.

In addition to the pills Emanuel had given to Big Mix, he'd passed off $500,000 in cash that was supposed to have gone to Mr. Raymond the same evening. However, things didn't go strictly to the plan like it should have. Big Mix was to have made a pit stop by his own place to temporarily drop off the pills to prevent from being dirty while driving, as he was to have taken the journey to Mr. Raymond's home. Once Mr. Raymond had the money, Mix was to then report back home, retrieve the pills yet again, then hit the road, enroute up the interstate to the motel where he had to await the customer who bought the narcotics. The reason why the plan hadn't gone accordingly, was due to Big Mix suffering from a case of sleep apnea. He'd dozed off to sleep and awakened hours later and began the drive to Pompano.

Roland continued. "You gave up a lot of information from your phone too, my nigga. Thanks! We appreciate that." The ridicule of Big Mix seemed unending.

"Like I told you . . . y'all dead, nigga. I promise you that," Big Mix retorted once again. He spit a thick glob of blood from his mouth.

"In case you were wondering, I don't plan to kill you. Not yet at least. I benefit more by you being alive than I do if you were a dead man. Besides, I want to have the pleasure to track your fuck ass down again. At some point in the future . . . then, kidnap you and rob you for all you got. How does that sound?" The taunts continued.

Chapter 6

The goons held Big Mix hostage for the next three days to follow. He was beaten, deprived of food and water, urinated on by Roland's pet Rottweilers, then dumped out along a railroad track in a desolated area off 12th Avenue heading north. A freight train conductor found him and called the paramedics for help. Mix seriously needed medical attention. He was near death. Not for once did he have any idea as to who were the perpetrators who abducted him, took what he had, broke into his house, then assaulted him. This proved to be a smooth robbery and attack.

Roland eventually reported back to his uncle, Mitch, to inform him on all that went down. He also had to turn over the pills and the money they'd hit for.

Mitch owned a luxurious, two-story mini mansion located in the Hialeah section of town. He and a girlfriend of his shared the home. The money utilized to buy the estate was made through the club he once part owned, King of Dimez. Just over two and a half million was paid over a three-year time period.

Mitch welcomed Roland inside. He and a few other male family members were there having a discussion about business-related matters. No time was wasted in getting to the news that Roland was looking to convey.

"Nephew," Mitch greeted with a smile. He and the others were seated at the thirteen chair, glass dining table in the dining room when Roland appeared. He was let in by the butler. "How you been? Here, have a drink. Let us know all about the successful mission you and your boys completed not long ago." Mitch poured up a glass of wine for Roland and proposed a toast.

"Oh, yeah. Let's do that, shall we, Unc? What we drinking on?" Roland responded.

"You already know I'm a wine type of nigga, nephew. We gonna drink from this here bottle of ninety-four-point Super Tuscan Saracosa," Mitch stated, pouring more portions into everyone's glasses and sliding them down the length of the table to each person.

Roland produced the duffle bag for Mitch, the one with the money in it. There was a total of $700,000 now, counting the additional $200,000 taken from Big Mix's place of residence.

"Unc, that tracking device shit worked to perfection. You know exactly how to locate and keep tabs on niggaz, don't you? I had to get a little crafty myself though, to trick the nigga to come out the motel room. But nonetheless, we got his ass," Roland related with a laugh. "I got something for you too. Here you go," he let out, tossing the bag full of cash over to his uncle.

"Well, I be damned!" Mitch exclaimed with a huge smile. "How much we got here?" he inquired, looking to take the words of the nephew at face value.

"A half-million. The nigga had about four hundred thousand pills too. Different types of many kinds. They were in the back of the truck stashed away in dark-colored, plastic clothing bins. More than likely, he was on the way to drop them off to somebody. The tracking device helped us know where he lived. That's where the money was found."

"That sounds about right on how that slimy-ass nigga, Raymond, operates. Mix must was in the process of doing one of three things. He was either waiting on customers from out of state to arrive, was intent on heading farther up the highway at daybreak to deliver the package. or, was looking to put the product away in a storage unit there for a few days until told otherwise what to do. But no matter what the nigga's intention *was* to do, we intercepted the play and took what he had," Mitch said. "Now that's gangsta!" He smiled widely, teeth showing, and he was full of jubilee. He was happy to have orchestrated a profitable revenge strike against Mr. Raymond. He continued. "This ain't the end of our attacks either. Ray owes me way more money than this, and I plan to get every penny of it. But anyway . . . count out a hundred and fifty thousand of those pills for you and your boys to keep." He then also dug into the duffle bag and pulled out stacks of $100 bills. They had labels of $10,000 on each. "Here. Take fifty thousand too. Split it between you and the crew."

"Thanks, Unc. I love you, my nigga," Roland responded.

"I love you too, nephew."

"Okay. So, look. Question. Once I get our portions of the pills, what am I to do with the rest of them?" Roland asked.

"Just hold on to them until I let you know who I'll need you to meet up with to give 'em to. Most likely, I'll have my guy, Nate, link up with you for them. He'll be sure to spread them out to the street teams, and everybody'll get rid of them like that, you know?" Mitch informed.

"No doubt. I'll do that, Unc."

"Oh, yeah. Another thing, nephew. Your uncle almost back in business with my own club this time."

"Word?! That's what's up. And if you rolling on an independent basis this time around, you ain't gonna have to go through the bullshit again," Roland said.

"I'm definitely going about this the right way for my second-class act. It's family only! That's it. This what we're here discussing now," Mitch related, waving a hand toward his two cousins.

"That's right, fam," one of the men stated.

"We here, family," declared the second.

Chapter 7

Mitch proceeded in speaking. "So, you see, the bond between me and Ray was something that went back years before we put the money together to buy the club. But I guess it don't matter who a nigga is to the next man or how long they've been in the game working alongside one another. Some motherfuckas simply don't have eternal loyalty running through their blood, nephew. And from what I now know, Ray-Ray, is one of those types of motherfuckas," Mitch stated with a bit of vehemence to his voice.

"I can understand you on that, Uncle Mitch. If anybody, you would be one of those men to know dude better than almost anybody else."

"But anyway, look, nephew, let me bring you up to par on where we are in conversation if you will . . . ." Mitch continued with the conversation.

The men discussed all the information and other revelations they'd discovered from the data of Big Mix's cell phone. Mix almost never deleted anything as he worked hard daily to try and be precise and particular with all his dealings and business affairs.

The type of pick-ups and deliveries that Big Mix had the duty to perform had occurred many times prior to. Not once had he suffered any interference on any accord by goons who were looking to rob him, let alone, kidnap, beat, and rob him in the fashion that Roland and his comrades had carried out. Atop of that, the goons had broken into his house, ransacked the place, and destroyed everything that was inside. Mr. Raymond's money was taken and the other valuables Big Mix owned. If anything, Big Mix now had some explaining to do, being he failed to follow the protocol and go about doing things like he was supposed to have done.

For one, Big Mix was supposed to have delivered Mr. Raymond the $500,000 in cash the exact same hour upon picking up the dough from Emanuel. That didn't happen. For another, he had strict instructions to call Mr. Ray and verbally announce that, indeed, he had the paper and the materials that came along with it. He failed to do so. Big Mix knew that his boss would probably find it hard to believe the story behind everything that had happened to him.

He was well aware that Mr. Ray had a thorough knowledge of how smart he was and of how steeped in matters of security he'd risen to, simply to have allowed anyone to follow him the full distance from Miami to Pompano, then take him hostage. But the tracking device ploy that Roland put to use for Mitch, was the thing Big Mix knew nothing about. Therefore, without that knowledge, all of the mirror watching and excessive detouring he'd done before exiting Miami's city limits, was to no avail. Big Mix didn't feel the need to relate this portion of the story. No matter how much truth there was to it.

Big Mix became plagued with a number of issues to come along in the aftermath of the caper that was pulled on him. The trust and reliability Mr. Ray had in him stood the risk of being damaged. No matter what had taken place, the man's money and narcotics had to be replaced. The cell phone taken from him was the only one that had a contact to Mr. Raymond. Big Mix couldn't dare appear at Mr. Raymond's home unannounced. This had never happened. And now that the opposition had his phone and acquired a treasure trove of information from it, this placed the entire enterprise in a compromising position moving forward. Nothing would remain the same.

Chapter 8

Presently . . .

A friend of Parlay's, a guy by the name of Fredrick, aka "Fred," aka "Four-Pound," was a high-ranking gang member within the world of the Bloods. He'd previously done a stretch in the Florida Department of Corrections, the place where he was initiated into the gang and embraced the culture of it all. Four-Pound (as he preferred to be addressed now) earned his stains in rank and had cultivated a solid bond with certain brethren on the inside. His ambition and drive propelled him to the top, making for him and the other "big homies" to lean upon one another for huge favors. Now free, Four-Pound found himself in one of those situations where he needed a sure helping hand. He had access to one of his highly ranked brothers of the order (as they called it). The two stayed connected through social media. The brother, who was still locked up, owned a contraband cell phone.

Jeffery Green, aka "Boskoe-Shine," was a "double OG" and called shots like the "big dawg" he claimed to be. They both represented the G-Shine set of the group.

It was Four-Pound who was the one to reach out to Boskoe by way of Messenger inbox. He left a phone number for him to text or call. Not long from the point of contact, Boskoe took notice of the message that awaited him.

Oh, okay. This the number to one of my homies. This my nigga, Four-Pound, here. He want me to get at him, he thought. "That's a bet," Boskoe expressed audibly in soliloquy. He texted Four-Pound a reply.

BOSKOE: *Yo, Dawg! Buss back at me. This Boskoe as you know already. 305-904-3855*

Four-Pound received the reply. He next made the call.

"Bang-Bang!" Boskoe answered.

"Yo, what's poppin',' Blood?" Four-Pound responded.

"I'm Bloody as always, Blood. What's poppin' on your end though?" asked Boskoe.

"We bangin' big B's on this end, for real, Blood! Only in a more sophisticated way now, you feel me?"

"No doubt, I do. But listen, Blood. I need a *favor!*" stated Four-Pound with much emphasis to the last word, apparently code for something else.

"Oh! One of *them*?!" responded Boskoe.

"One of *them*, my nigga! And the work I need done, so happen to be on the end where you and your young scraps at. And once this gets done, I'll see to it with the dawgs out here that we reward everybody with big dawg stains up in there. That's on Blood, we will," stated Four-Pound.

"Word!"

"Motherfuckin' word, dawg!"

"So, what the lick read, Blood? Who we got on the plate?" Boskoe inquired.

"I'll text you the toe tag from a different line, Blood. The nigga who's the topic of the discussion had hurt my goddaughter. He likes to molest little girls and think shit sweet," Four-Pound stated.

"What?! Say no more, Blood. Whoever this nigga is, he a dub now. We gonna eat that fool!" Boskoe declared emphatically.

"Yeah. Y'all cancel that nigga's party for good. He don't need no more special days. Be sure that it's *over* for him." Four-Pound stated the specifics of how he wanted the guy to be punished.

The conversation came to an end. Shortly thereafter, Boskoe received the text message he awaited. All the particulars were included. He wasted no time getting to work in gaining allocation on the dormitory where the marked man was being housed. Boskoe needed to look no further than to the PREA/sex offender dorm there at the prison, being that the information made it clear on who he was and what he was locked up for. A Blood gang hit team was assembled. Boskoe led the pack.

Chapter 9

The time was 5:00 P.M. when the three-member relentless goon squad went to take care of the business at hand. The intended victim, Charles Griffen, had just awakened and was busy brushing his teeth in his cell to prepare for breakfast as the shank carrying assassins ran in on him. The first to enter, Boskoe, was the most physically fit and the most aggressive of the trio. He punched Charles dead square in the nose, knocking him to the back wall of the room. Boskoe then rushed him and placed the frantic guy in a chokehold maneuver from behind, cutting short the oxygen supply to the man's body. He had a few words for Charles in the process.

"Yeah, motherfucka! You wanna go around and rape little girls and then think you can get away with it unpunished! Nah, nigga! You had that wrong. Your ass gonna die today, fuck boy!" the *brolic* goon, Boskoe, had stated.

The other two who assisted then began to viciously stab Charles all about the body, without the slightest show of mercy. They plunged the sharp pointed weapons deep into the torso of the sex offending perp. Charles squirmed in a vehement manner, attempting to break free from Boskoe's clutch. He had no luck with doing so. The hitters had him down badly that morning. His fate was sealed. He was ordained to die this day.

Charles was hit thirty plus times with the shanks with several of those thrusts striking the heart. His body dangled lifelessly in the chokehold position he was still being held in. Finally, Boskoe allowed the dead man to drop to the floor. The other assailants ripped the pants from him. A thick wooden broom handle was at the ready. It was about two feet in length. Boskoe grabbed hold of it then rammed it into the anus of Charles roughly fifteen times prior to stopping with the malicious act of sodomy. Before making their escape, the broom handle was left in place, deep into the rectum of the murdered man. They'd tossed the body onto the bed and covered him with bed sheets. The roommate of his was gone to the medical window for pill call. He was an elder white male. There was a huge surprise awaiting him upon his return.

There was no one to bear witness to the three killers enter the dorm, locate Charles' cell, go hit him, and exit with no problem. And even so if there had been, a "rapist" or a "child molester", as was Charles, wasn't cared for by anyone, or on any level. Not even by fellow convicts with the same offenses. The essential "g-code" and "no snitching" policy of the chain gang had won the day. Although the prison was placed on lockdown for a day or so as the investigation ensued, no one became a suspect, and no one folded and spoke out about the incident. Life continued to move on. Charles was no more.

—

The daughter of Parlay was in her last year of college. She was back home in Miami on break and made it her business to stop by her grandmother's place to visit. Her father was there as well. The two were seated in the living room, enjoying snacks and having a meaningful conversation while the grandmom was in the kitchen preoccupied with baking a cake for the granddaughter, Sherita. Her special day was the Saturday approaching. It was a Thursday.

One day before this, Parlay received a text message from the homie of his, Four-Pound. There was good news to be reported. The mark who he wanted taken out, was tagged and zipped in a body bag. Parlay was confident in knowing that Four-Pound would make it happen. Of all people. And now, he had confirmation to how official his homie really was in the Blood gang he represented. He'd called a shot and had the guy, Charles, whacked.

The TV was on. Parlay's mother always let it remain on the local news channel around this time of day. It was 6:00 P.M. A specific report came across from the news center, one which was of interest to Parlay:

"The Florida Department of Corrections reported the death of an inmate who was housed at the Florida State Prison. The body of forty-nine-year-old Charles Griffen was discovered two days ago by facility staff, the DOC reported. He was apparently stabbed multiple times then placed in his bunk inside the cell with the blanket drawn over to conceal. A really bizarre twist was attached to the crime. Griffen's body had a wooden handle from a broom plunged into the anus by force. It remained in place by the attackers until the body was eventually found. There stands no witnesses to the violent incident, and no suspects have been named. Charles Griffen was serving time for rape, child molestation, and sodomy. The prison was placed on lockdown until the investigation was completed. I'm Jeremy Lumpkin reporting on the crime."

"Daddy! Daddy! That was him! That was Charles! He's the bastard who hurt me!" Parlay's daughter yelled out at her observance of the photo and mention of the name on the TV screen. She appeared shocked and yet relieved. Her view was that justice had been served.

"Oh, that was the clown, baby?!" Parlay responded. He'd seen the photo too.

"Yes, Daddy. That was him. My momma's so-called husband. Somebody killed him in the prison he was in. That's good for his behind, too," Sherita stated. The relief of emotion streamed down her face with the tears. She leaned over and wrapped her arms around her father's body, burying her face into his shirt. It became soaked with the tears that poured forth. "Yes, Daddy. That's the bastard. I'm glad he's now dead. I'm so glad. Now, he won't be able to hurt nobody else," she stated, expressing emphasis in how relieved she now was.

"It's okay, baby. It's okay now. Go ahead and let it all out. You can. It's okay," Parlay said to his daughter. His words were comforting.

The two maintained a tight embrace for a prolonged period of time. He assured her that it would be over his dead body before he blew the chance again to remain by her side and protect her like he was supposed to throughout the rest of her life.

"Daddy, you've got to promise me, dude, that you're gonna stay out of trouble and keep on being free," Sherita demanded.

"Baby, I promise you . . . Daddy promise you . . .that I'm gonna stay out of trouble and keep free, okay?" he stated then planted a kiss of confidence on her forehead following his words.

Parlay now had the duty to do all in his power to keep his word to his one and only. This may prove to be a difficult task, no doubt.

Chapter 10

Following the months' long connection that was maintained between the owner of Love Dolls Gentlemen's club and Special Agent Ursula Corbin, aka "Yolanda Harris", aka "Yola Sweets", (unbeknownst to Rich, the club owner and night life mogul), per direct order from the superiors, she was pulled from the case she'd been working, and told to vacate Miami. This was to be a temporary occurrence. Agent Corbin, was instructed to return home, to the state of Virginia, for safety and security purposes, and not to return to Miami until further notice. The reason for a suspension of the case was due to a drastic change in planning and strategy on how to take down the Raymond Stephens organization.

The rift between he and Mitch, and the conflict that ensued, complicated the investigation. Certain matters of concern came about, mostly due to the primary target—Mr. Raymond—suddenly abandoning the clubbing business and extricating himself from his previous activities of the underworld, to pursue a late career in politics. He now held ambition and desire to be the mayor of Miami, running on the Republican ticket.

There became the need for the government to begin conducting separate investigations of the two subjects—Mr. Raymond and Mitch. After the sale of the club they owned together, the trail got cold in many areas, and the planted mole had no abilities to further penetrate the areas of weaknesses as once before. The government didn't feel they had enough to proceed with to obtain an indictment and prosecute. The investigation needed to continue. New material was necessary; that way, the charges would stick, and the powerful street dons could take a hard fall from grace and be put away in prison for a long time to come.

Mr. Raymond proceeded as he were, with might and main. He made it his top priority to terminate all previous contracts that everyone employed at the club once held. He also killed the communications that they once had to access him directly. This included the information that Yolanda had as well. The intimate details she provided from the steep position once held was compromised. She was stripped of this when Mr. Raymond sold King of Dimez.

Mr. Raymond once attempted to impress Yolanda, by bragging about how he'd made $3M in seventeen days from the items that the club sold. He showered her with special attention. Mr. Raymond also went so far as to offer to buy Yolanda all that she asked of him, if she were to give in and become a mistress of his. The thirst for her was immense. But no matter how hard he tried to woo her to gravitate toward him in the way he so desired, she had to refuse all of his advances. For good cause over time, Mr. Raymond put a stop to seeking Yolanda in this type of way and simply maintained a business rapport. This served him better in regards to her.

Yolanda held an interest in the club prior to its sale. This had nothing to do with any of the underworld affairs that Mr. Raymond had in progress with the drug crew he operated. She'd been brought onboard by Mr. Raymond, and the only thing she and Mitch had in common was a business relationship. However, there was dirt on him too. And the mission of the FBI regarding this case was to take them both down. Special Agent Corbin, operating as Yolanda, wasn't able to turn up any serious evidence to warrant immediate unsealing of an indictment and arrest. And the government, didn't want to continue with risking her life being endangered by any means. This was why the suspension was ordered, and she pulled from the case. It was for proper rest, security, and to allow for a regroup.

On the flip side to that, SA Corbin, was inadvertently connected to another serious case that originated in the state of Texas. The missing friend of hers, Rachel, provided damning evidence to her about the ex-boyfriend in the Midwest, a guy by the name of Santino Bodaford, aka "S Bubbs." The material was submitted to FBI field offices with proper jurisdiction to handle the case. And with Rachel no longer around and presumed dead, the evidence could become too weak to prosecute, especially without the key witness, someone who the agent had grown fond of and loved dearly. The thoughts of Rachel caused her to cry. Nonetheless, life must go on, and SA Corbin made a vow to herself to see to it that the ex-boyfriend was eventually arrested and brought to justice for the crimes she was to level against him.

—

Mr. Raymond eventually made his return from the extended vacation he'd taken to Turks and Caicos then to Cancun, Mexico. Another trip was in the making, one which would include the nephew of his, the person who was selected to succeed him in the underworld, Philip Stephens Jr, aka "Lil Phil."

Mr. Raymond found himself highly pissed at Big Mix. He wasn't answering his phone. He hadn't delivered the cash to him like he was supposed to have and didn't meet up with the customers of his who'd travelled to South Florida to purchase the large quantity of pills they'd put in an order for. Not a word was shared by Mr. Raymond to anyone about Big Mix's absence other than with Emanuel. He hadn't seen or heard from Big Mix either from the time he passed over to him the money and the pills. He needed to show his face and explain why he'd failed to properly carry out his business duties.

Mr. Raymond's other bodyguard, the most trusted and committed one, Willie, was still away in New York City, accompanying Mr. Raymond's wife and daughter, Christine and Erin, on their shopping spree. He always sent the two away any time he had pressing business to deal with, or, whenever he desired to roam around Miami loosely with one of the other females he dealt with, like Felicia perhaps.

Christine was no fool by any measure. She knew that her husband was an unfaithful man. She also had knowledge about the females he carried on affairs with. One in particular was Felicia, and the bank statements to the account that they shared revealed this. A $50K financial transaction was made to her. It was marked as a "miscellaneous reimbursement" payment to a Felicia Nicole Blount.

Christine immediately got busy with her research to know more about the woman who her husband "paid back" $50,000 to. Her social media profiles were discovered. Felicia updated and stayed active on a daily basis. She'd even went so far as to post the photos online that she and Mr. Raymond took together while on vacation. He was completely oblivious to her putting those pictures out to the public. Christine was furious but held her composure. Her way to retaliate was to seek a divorce. Also, there was a need to shield their sixteen-year-old daughter from the foul behavior that her father was putting on display.

The cartel leader who Mr. Raymond was supplied by, a Mr. Ramirez Chucho, was provided assurance by Mr. Raymond, that the person who he was to handpick to succeed him, would be installed and in place very soon so that their drug business could continue. Mr. Raymond had to pause for a true cause. He'd filed all the official documentations that was necessary to begin his candidacy for mayor. The pact that the two had made—Mr. Raymond and Mr. Chucho—was long established that once the operations were to get underway, Mr. Raymond would be in it for life. And Mr. Chucho offered no way out. Mr. Raymond now knew entirely too much about him for this to take place. The threat of him and his entire family being annihilated loomed if he attempted to exit the life and break the agreement which they had. Mr. Raymond swore with his life and that of his family when initiated into the order with the cartel that he wouldn't abandon his post. What followed was an increase in drug supply to Mr. Raymond, courtesy of Mr. Chucho, and elevating Mr. Raymond to a totally different tax bracket. He was grateful. He also owed a debt that could only be paid in blood. And now, by those 400,000 pills being missing, along with a half million in cash, this put Mr. Raymond behind in a troubling way, leaving Big Mix to answer up to the mishap.

Chapter 11

With no way to contact Mr. Raymond other than by physically appearing at the man's home, he had no choice but to make this the only route to take to explain what all had happened to him. Big Mix had regained his strength and his mind. Although without a vehicle he owned any longer, he withdrew funds from his bank account, rented a moving truck to relocate from where he previously lived, and also rented a small car to get around in. He finally made the drive to Mr. Raymond's home to show his face and reveal his troubles.

He knocked on the front door upon arrival. The Spanish housekeeper answered then notified Mr. Raymond of the visitor.

"Jerome!" Mr. Raymond let out. He had an angry tone to his voice.

"Mr. Ray. Please forgive me. But I got some awfully bad news," Big Mix responded. He was welcomed inside.

"Jerome! Take a good look at me. You see how happy and relieved that I find myself. Does it look like I want to be presented with any bad news? As you already are aware, I care nothing for excuses. So don't even waste your time giving me one," Mr. Raymond stated.

"Mr. Ray, if you will, please let me explain. I can provide an understand—"

"An understanding, you were about to say?" Mr. Raymond cut Big Mix's words short to express. "The only understanding that I've come to is one with myself. Because Jerome, you failed me. And that's all I know when it comes to you at this point. You let me down."

"Mr. Ray, I was hit in the head, kidnapped, held hostage, and robbed for all I had," Big Mix revealed. "Take a look at my head here," he said, pointing with a forefinger at the large wounds he had about his head. Multiple staples were used to close them. "Those motherfuckas hit me on my head with some heavy, hard object. I was knocked out for a while."

"So, where were my pills located when all of this was going on?"

"I had them in the back of my truck. It was late in the night when this happened. I was in the motel room resting up for the next day to complete the deals for you," Big Mix explained.

"And what about my money? Why didn't you bring it by the house and give it to Elonor like you were instructed to do?" Mr. Raymond drilled with harder questions.

"I figured that it was okay to wait until I returned back here to Miami to do so once I'd completed the business with the pills."

"Those were not my instructions, Jerome. Now, were they?" Mr. Raymond retorted. "I specifically told you exactly how I wanted you to handle things. Did I not?"

"Yes. You did, Mr. Ray. But I—"

"But I, my ass, Jerome!" Mr. Raymond cut him off again to say, "We've done this far too many times for you to not go according to the plan, big fella. And why didn't you immediately contact me the very moment those goons set you free?" Mr. Raymond demanded to know.

"Mr. Ray, all the contact information I had to you was saved in my phone. That was taken too. I couldn't remember any of your numbers by heart," Big Mix replied.

"So, why couldn't you just make it your business to come by the house like you've done just now? Elenor could've easily called me for you," Mr. Raymond uttered. Big Mix remained silent now behind the reprimand. "And you never said where you had my money situated. You skipped over that part."

"I left the money at my house in the bedroom closet," responded Big Mix.

Mr. Raymond paused for a moment to ponder on the words Big Mix spoke. "Jerome, help me understand this, will you?"

"I'll do my best, Mr. Ray."

"Please explain to me exactly how did the guys who kidnapped you in Pompano also know where you lived in Miami, to break in and rob you for the money too?" Mr. Raymond asked.

"Mr. Ray, to be honest with you, sir, I have no idea. Your guess is just as good as mine. I don't know where to begin explaining that."

Whether or not Big Mix spoke the truth to Mr. Raymond, his explanation didn't appear to come across as a convincing one. Mr. Raymond voiced this to Big Mix with the following. "Jerome, I've got to be straight up with you, my man. I find your story one to be very hard to believe," he stated emphatically. The two men continued to lock eyes and stare at one another in a menacing way now. Tension filled the air. Big Mix felt he was being blatantly made out to be a liar. He expressed his thoughts without biting his tongue.

"Mr. Ray, as many times as I've put my life on the line to defend and safeguard you and your family, how dare you question me and my word about being kidnapped and robbed for a batch of pills and a stash of penny ante cash? My loyalty and integrity should mean more to you than what you're showing me."

"Jerome, the loss of four hundred thousand pills and a half million bucks of my money . . . that's more than enough reason to *not* trust you any longer or believe anything that you may say," Mr. Raymond retorted. He'd never spoken so seriously to Big Mix before in all their years of being tied together.

Big Mix maintained a stern gaze at Mr. Raymond. He was motionless and at a loss of words to rebut what had been cast at him. The only thing he could manage to say was the obvious to come to mind. "Mr. Ray, I could've been killed by those dudes over those pills. My two daughters were on the verge of being without a father. I've put everything on the line time and time again for you. I've even done unspeakable things without once questioning, all because you told me to do so. My conscience gets the best of me every so often behind the fact that I took the life of a young mother to be, all because you didn't want it to get out that you was the father of the girl's unborn. You didn't want the affair y'all had to become known to your wife. That shit, of all things, haunts me most. And now, you gonna stand your ass here, look me in my eyes, and tell me to my motherfuckin' face that you find my story hard to believe. Nigga! There's something terribly wrong with you, Ray! I used to not believe a thing Mitch used to say about you. But now, I ain't got no choice but to believe every word that the man has said about you. You're foul, homeboy! For real you are!" Big Mix lastly stated in his long-winded rant.

The surprise to this was the fact that Mr. Raymond afforded him the opportunity to say all of the above and not cut him off in doing so.

Big Mix turned to walk out the door. Mr. Raymond, fuming with anger and resentment, absolutely could not allow a worker of his to say all he had then exit on him without having the last word.

"You ain't heard the last of me, Jerome. My money and my product meant something to me. And I promise you, I'm gonna get down to the bottom of it. You'll have hell to pay if I find out you stole from me. Absolute hell to pay, Jerome. Trust and believe that," Mr. Raymond stated to him.

Big Mix continued to walk toward the car, not threatened by his words. He took them lightly. Maybe he shouldn't have.

Chapter 12

Before Calvin was to be allowed release from the hospital, the police needed to run him through a series of questions pertaining to the shooting incident he was the victim of. He was shown the surveillance footage of him entering the Popeye's Chicken restaurant, footage of him inside and other areas of the dining section, and footage of him making an exit. He was also shown certain footage of the restaurant and a few patrons who'd visited just prior to him arriving. Several still photos were captured from the filming of others who showed up before he had, and they were presented.

"Mister Prescott, please take a good look at the photos and footage for us. Are you sure you don't recognize any of the faces of the few people who entered and/or exited prior to or after you? Perhaps someone who you passed on your way out or encountered while placing your order?" the detective, Dana Clements, asked of him.

Calvin looked on at the video and pictures long and hard in an effort to identify any of the individuals or something about them to make connection to who it was attempting to take his life. "No, sir. I don't recognize anyone other than the girl, Shonda, there," he pointed out with a forefinger, "who took my order. But if possible, can I see the video from the drive thru again?" he requested.

"Sure. No problem," responded the detective. He showed Calvin the particular portion that he asked for.

"Detective," Calvin called out. "I got a quick question to ask."

"And what's that, Mister Prescott?"

"I'm not a fool by any stretch of the imagination. And, I know for a fact that I ain't the only nigga who done got shot in the past two weeks. This Miami, Florida! A city that thrives on violence. There's even violent video games to demonstrate this fact that's based in Miami. But what I wanna know is, why are y'all so concerned about solving this particular shooting over all the others? And I ain't die?!"

The question prompted the investigator to jar his head and look on at the wounded victim in a perplexing way. Normally, people who were shot never posed such penetrating questions. Calvin, on the other hand, wasn't someone who would allow the obvious to pass him by.

"That's a good question, Mister Prescott. I thought you'd never ask. But if you must know . . . those bullets you were hit with . . ." he began.

"Yeah. What about those bullets I was hit with?" Calvin now inquired.

"They were high grade, Navy Seal, military issue only bullets. *Gecko* hollow points. Also known as 'cop killer' on the streets. Those are some baaad boys! They destroy everything in their path. That's why you had to have so many surgeries, Mister Prescott. They'd damaged your spleen, your liver, your left lung, and blew a hole in your gut. I'm surprised that we're even talking now. Your ass is supposed to be dead already. I'm only stating the facts for you, Mister Prescott. It's a damn shame, but more than likely, you've probably got to wear a colostomy bag for the remainder of your life. And you'll never have full use of your left arm and leg again. But back to what I was originally saying. We checked into your background and discovered that you have a history in gun trafficking. Maybe it was somebody from your past who'd taken aim at you. We're trying to narrow the investigation as best we could," the detective stated.

"Damn. I was beginning to wonder why I had to stay at the hospital here for as long as I've been here," Calvin let out.

"Well . . . now you know. There you have it," Mr. Clements acknowledged. "Now, my next question to you, Mister Prescott, is why would someone be gunning to kill you? No pun intended. But they wanted you dead! And they used sophisticated means in trying to carry out the mission."

"What you mean by that?" Calvin chimed in to ask.

"It's because, the gun that was used; It was an automatic. All those rounds that were fired, and not one shell casing was found. The car you were shot in . . . was riddled by bullets. There should have been at least one shell casing left around. Not any."

"Oh! Wow! I would've thought the same myself. But you say there was none. That means it was an attempted hit?" asked Calvin.

"Apparently so. I'm simply trying to determine if or not the shooting wasn't any act of retaliation. Do you owe someone money, Mister Prescott? Have you offended the wrong person? Did you do something to piss someone off? The reason I ask is because, the theory to surround the investigation is that the assailant may try to double back to get you for real a second time. And the commissioner of the police department, is hot on our asses behind four homicides in the last sixty days that involved cop killer Gecko bullets, the ones used in an attack to attempt at making *you*, the fifth murder victim behind them," stated the detective emphatically.

"This sounds way more serious than I initially thought," Calvin responded.

"That's because, it is, Mister Prescott. Hell . . . those types of bullets you were hit with, we—the police—don't even have authority to be issued, not even for tactical situations. Say if a heavy bank robbery were to occur, and the perps are wearing full body armor, we'd need proper ammo like those Geckos to penetrate their covering."

"That's understood, sir. But if you don't mind, may I take another look at those photos and footage once more? In particular, those of the people eating inside the restaurant please, sir," Calving requested.

The detective was delighted to accommodate him with what he'd asked.

As Calvin reviewed the photos yet again, there was something that stood out completely to him regarding a person captured in the picture. It was a guy who was seated at a table eating. He had on a dark blue and orange colored Boise State University snap back football hat that was pulled low. It was apparently to cover his face for whatever reason. Nonetheless, this was bad table manners. Hats were not to be worn at a table at any time, especially while someone was eating.

But, Calvin knew only one person in the world, who had a crazy sincere love and passion to favor a team that was way out in Idaho over the many beloved schools he could do the same for there in the state of Florida, not to mention, having an obsession for a football team above that of the Miami Hurricanes. There was only one person he knew who loved the Boise State football team, but happened to be born and raised in Miami, and that was none other than Melvin Anderson, aka Parlay. This was the guy who he—Calvin— had ratted out to the police, then came the Feds where he eventually did the same thing, and lastly, testified on the man in trial, helping him get convicted and put away in prison for nearly two decades.

Could it be Melvin? He's the only one I know, of all the people I know, who love Boise State. Nah. it can't be him. I'm sure he's got a few more years to do in prison. And the guy in the photo here, he's got a full beard and way too buffed with muscle to be Melvin. It can't be him. But, I'mma be sure to check more into it sometime soon so I'll know, Calvin thought.

Calvin shook his head at the detective. "No, sir, Mister Clements. I don't seem to recognize no one in the photos or videos, even after a second attempt to do so. Not right off. But at the same time, I am under a heavy dosage of pain medication. And I may not be at full strength mentally. I am somewhat drowsy. But once I'm properly able to focus and think, I'll be able to assist you better at that time," Calvin stated to the cop.

"Not a problem, Mister Prescott. And I'm more than sure that you want the guy put away yourself who tried to end your life."

"In a major way. But we gotta first find out who he was. Just leave me your card and I'll be sure to get back to you soon, okay?"

"That'll work, Mister Prescott. That'll work, sir," Detective Clements lastly responded, passing Calvin a contact card and departing the hospital room.

Calvin remained lying on the bed, closed his eyes, and began to think deeply over everything from the night he was shot. He sought to know who it was that possibly wanted him dead. The intention was to narrow it down to a few, if not one in particular.

Chapter 13

Parlay and his cousin, Vick, found themselves out and about again, cruising about town. This was the usual routine at any time the two had something serious to be discussed. Vick was the one to initiate the talk. It surrounded the importance of what he currently had going on.

"Parlay, me and my boys got a few planned trips to the north coming up soon. And I mentioned to you before that I've got my own team in place now. That way, there won't be any trust issues to deal with. Like me, the dudes who's with me, they've got a lot to lose too. But eventually, it's gonna be nothing but family I'm getting the money with. It's been a minute since we last talked about all this I'm looking to do and the level of business we're intent on handling. So, what's up? You rolling with me, or you not? Because, I can definitely use you, fam," Vick stated to him.

"I been thinking long and hard over everything that we once had a conversation about. I certainly wanna get back in the game and hustle by selling the guns and all else. That's all I know. But I don't wanna be involved on a full-time basis. I still got other options to explore and possibly dabble into. And my mind is fixed on exercising all money-making routes that I got at my disposal. But to answer your question specifically, I'm in, cuz. I'm with you, fam. It's obvious to me that you know what you're doing. I know I'll be in good hands. After all these years and you ain't never gotten knocked, you got a license to carry guns how you see fit, and you're a registered member of the NRA. How could I go wrong with you leading the way? I only had to get over the fear factor first that I once faced when I got out. And I promised my mom, my daughter, and my girlfriend, Traci, that I wouldn't get into any more trouble. I can't allow myself to let them down, fam. I absolutely can't," Parlay said to Vick in a clear and understandable tone of voice.

"Cuz, listen. If you think negative, you get negative. If you think positive, you'll get positive. My point is that, since you're now back in the game, you don't need to bring nothing but the correct type of energy with you to get the right type of results. You feel me?" responded Vick.

"True on that, fam. But you gotta understand where I'm coming from too, Vick."

"Parlay, I clearly understand where you're coming from, my nigga. You just served almost twenty years in prison. And, you don't wanna go back. How hard could it be to understand that shit?! Or, as you put it, to *feel you* on that?! I do. I empathize with you on all that, cuz. Didn't I support you the whole time you were gone?"

"No doubt, you did," Parlay replied.

"Well then, nigga. There you go. We both made our point felt," Vick further expounded.

Parlay was able to properly communicate to his cousin that he was eager to get back involved with the business of gun trafficking, and he also made him aware that he only wanted his involvement to be on a limited basis. Throughout the conversation, Parlay's mind became flooded with numerous thoughts of potential issues or dilemmas that may come about by signing back up to conduct illegal affairs. Some—he perceived—would naturally resolve themselves. And for the most complex of the bunch, he'd be compelled to eradicate on his own accord.

But, for the most part, the thing he had the hardest time grappling with since being free, was the fact of how lost and behind he was in regards to social interactions and on how to relate to common people in civil society. He'd suffered depravity on a high level behind all those years of being away in prison, and he struggled on many ends. However, he felt as though he was prepared to take on the challenges that lay ahead of him.

Also, Parlay hated the fact of not having the slightest clue in the universe on how to properly relate in a new world way with the young adult daughter of his. He felt that Sherita may have hated him for all the reasons she had and especially for him getting in trouble and not being present in her life to provide, protect, and to teach her as a real dedicated father should have been. Seventeen years removed from a person's life was a very long time. There was a huge gap that existed—one that was impossible to bridge, being that it was technically too late to do so. The man had missed out on everything. And now that he was free, Sherita was grown, and their period of separation was no more, but he struggled to pick up the pieces of a shattered relationship.

And so, Parlay found himself at the crossroads yet again. He had one leg in the game and the other on legitimate grounds. No matter how hard he fought not to, he found himself reverting to his old ways again by involving himself in illegal activities to gain a fast buck. And to make matters worse, he'd shot a man multiple times, almost taking the guy's life and possibly racking up a charge of murder. Parlay became a paranoid-schizophrenic. Each time he dwelled upon his current reality of who may get to him first—the police or Calvin Prescott—it made matters worse. Not to mention, there were the newly created enemies or those from his past who still may have desired to do him in. Things became hectic in a way for the man. There was a need to sort things out then proceed forward.

Chapter 14

Parlay's thoughts ran rampant over all he and Vick talked over a day prior to. *I ain't got no other skills to do nothing else. The streets and the hustle is all I know. So, fuck it! I may as well get back down and dirty. I ain't got but one life to live, so I might as well go on and live it to the fullest. On the edge too. I'm a livewire. I love the action. I love the streets. I love to be directly in the midst of shit. That's how I stay sharp. This is the lifestyle that keeps my wits stimulated and me on alert. At some point, I do plan to go all the way legit and have a business of my own. But in the meantime, I simply gotta play the hand that I'm dealt and do the best I can to come out on top and win the game I'm playing in.*

For the most part, the majority of men in American society had their sights set on gaining power, being dominant, and possessing the ability to control others. Basically, desiring to run shit and do what they wanted to do. Parlay, on this note, didn't know of one bona fide man that was sure of themselves who didn't wish for power. Not one. Therefore, the question for him came down to this: If anything, what was a man to do—himself per se—with the power that he had at the point of acquiring it? This was one of the main things he had to do, have an introspection with himself upon, and more than likely, a potential challenge he would undoubtedly face.

Throughout conversations he held with himself, he convinced his mind and spirit to believe that he was poised to take on such a match up as he performed his dance and parlayed his way to a position of power. He was hopeful that history had taught him a lesson on many things—most important, lessons about himself.

The two cousins felt the need to take another stroll through the city and talk over the game plan and strategy again, for the upcoming trips to the north they were set to make.

"So, Vick, give me a brief rundown on how the operation functions now. You know I'm behind like crazy, fam," Parlay asked his people to explain.

"It goes like this, cuz. I got people in positions in Louisiana, Alabama, Georgia, Tennessee, and South Carolina, who either own gun shops, or, got a team of motherfuckas that break into gun shops, pawn shops, or other sporting goods stores to get the goods. Some of the shit I get is hot. But for the most part, it's legit. I buy up everything on a wholesale basis, then turn and sell it on retail to my clientele base in the north. I get the best and most shit out of Georgia due to the lax gun laws that the peach state got. There's a lot of vulnerable shops there too. All over the place. When I get my calls and they tell me what they got, I evaluate the demand, and then, I make my purchase. I got two places in Georgia I make stops on my way up. That's in Savannah and in Atlanta, to do my buys. The reason these two spots are of importance is because they're a straight shot for me up the *Iron Pipeline*," Vick related.

"Oh! So now I know why they declare that particular route by such a name," Parlay responded.

"Now you know."

"I remember reading about the Iron Pipeline and gun trafficking in the Wall Street Journal. I also remember listening to a news segment on NPR's *All Things Considered* that discussed this."

"So, you did your homework too, I see," Vick let out.

"You got to know that, fam. I had to feed my mind with all things relevant to the game I know all too well. I'm versed on the subject. But anyway, look, cuz. Let's make a stop at one of those upscale bars I'm sure you're familiar with. I wanna puff on a premium cigar and get my drink on for a moment. My taste buds crave Dom. P," Parlay expressed.

"That's a bet, fam. We can do that. I got the urge to do the same thing."

Vick pushed the big body BMW 760Li toward the South Beach area. They both had the same thing in mind, splurge momentarily and flirt with the females that would be present.

Parlay's mind was totally made up at this point about his re-entry into the gun trafficking arena. He desired to win this time and vowed to not let anything or anyone come between his objectives. He'd put this on God that he wouldn't. The man was desperate and determined to know what it felt like to have a million dollars at his disposal.

There was no other option he knew of to get that kind of money. It was death and to the graveyard if all else failed. If anything, Parlay was confident that he'd done a good job spelling out things to Vick on how he was looking to move with him. Because truth be told, he really didn't have another prison bid left in him to do. It was death before dishonor for the man. There could be no recklessness in between.

Chapter 15

Mitch, the Haitian-American street boss, made it his business to have a conversation with his eldest daughter, Tisha. She was somebody who also operated as his accountant and safekeeper regarding a lot of valuable possessions and money he had. He stopped by her house this day to do so in person. Also, there was $300,000 in tow he wanted to put away. This was the lion's share of the cash that Big Mix was yanked for.

The second daughter of Mitch and Tisha's younger sister, Chioma, was there at Tisha's home with them. The two maintained a close bond. Chioma kept Tisha's two kids for her often times. There was a boy and a girl, little Sekou and Bella. A brief discussion was necessary as well regarding the hair and nail shop that he'd dumped heavy money into for his girls to have. The timing was perfect.

The father and two daughters sat in the living room while the kids remained in their rooms. Mitch initiated the conversation.

"Daddy always feels good about himself anytime I get the chance to talk with both my girls together," he said then hugged and kissed the two on the forehead. He sat between them on the couch.

"We feel the same way, Daddy," responded Tisha.

"Yeah, we love having our time spent with you too, Pop," Chioma chimed in to say.

"Okay, so Tisha, catch me up to date on how the business has been performing. Oh, and by the way, this is a conference. So, keep things in perspective from this point of view."

"Well, Daddy, as usual, the hair and nail salons have generated a good profit. We've managed to increase the wholesale market of the products that we offer. Our African suppliers provide greater opportunities too. The more money we spend, the more products that they discount in bulk, especially with the skin care items. Also, the human hair that we import from India and Indonesia for the wigs, the weaves, and the braids . . . We've increased the supply on those too. This is a booming market," Tisha revealed.

"This is a very good thing, baby. A very good thing. Just be sure to handle all the tax related documents properly, okay?" stated Mitch.

"Absolutely," replied Tisha.

"And Chioma, the other businesses you and your sister here got up and going for the family? The ones you supervise, the Laundromats and the vending machines. How's everything?"

"Everything is going good, Daddy. The Laundromats definitely. They were a great idea for you to get into. I keep in constant contact with the live-in maintenance tenants we got overseeing things. We keep the vending machines fully stocked and on time like we supposed to have them. The fragrance shop is doing well too. The girls that I have over the place are amazing." Chioma made her father aware.

"Me and Chioma got everything thriving and functioning well, Daddy. We're experiencing success by all measures," Tisha affirmed to keep Mitch confident in the work his girls were doing and his decision to put them in charge.

"I love the sound of all you two have shared with me, ladies," Mitch remarked with a bright smile.

"What about you, playboy? How's the club bid going?" inquired Tisha.

"Well . . . your daddy wasn't able to get the big space that I really wanted, but I did manage to get something negotiated."

"And that being?"

"I was able to persuade the owner of what used to be 'Club Ice,' to sell me the building," Mitch stated.

"Club Ice?!" asked Chioma.

Chapter 16

Mitch elaborated further. "Yeah. Club Ice. It was a popular hole in the wall strip club on Seventy-ninth and Seventh Avenue across from the Bays Inn motel, the Checkers, and the Bahamian Cafe there in the area. Down the road there, not too far from here."

Tisha's home was located in Little Haiti.

"Oh! You talking about the little blue building, right?" Tisha asked, now remembering the building he was referring to.

"Yeah, baby. That spot. Your daddy now owns it," Mitch confirmed.

"Well, congratulations, Daddy. You've worked hard to have your own spot. And now, you got it. But question. What's your plan with the building? What type of night-life haven are you intent on transforming the place into?" Tisha asked.

"I'm curious to know this myself," Chioma offered her input.

"If you two must know . . . I plan to have the building renovated and upgraded to a state-of-the-art social lounge slash gentlemen's club, to the best of my abilities," Mitch said to his daughters.

"What about the name? I'm hoping you do plan to change it. Don't you? Because we don't need our critiques and detractors trying to make your club synonymous with the drug, meth, by you keeping the name, Ice," Chioma implied with a serious tone to her voice.

"I'm telling you! Now that . . . we don't need," Tisha opined.

"Calm down, ladies, calm down, will you? I've already changed the name. It was only right that I do so," Mitch declared.

"To what?!" both Tisha and Chioma said seemingly at the same time.

"Y'all ready for this?"

"We are," the girls let out, once more together.

"I originally wanted to call it, King of Dames, because it was me who came up with the name of the club me and Ray owned together. And I didn't never get the credit for it. But, I backed away from that so to not have anything that I exclusively own to be associated in no type of way with what Ray had anything to do with. Therefore, I came to the conclusion to just simply call it—"

"Daddy, spit it out already, will you?" Chioma remarked.

"Club Pressure! How does that sound?" Mitch finally revealed.

"Club Pressure, huh? That's dope. Different too," Tisha said first.

"That's fly. How did you come up with that?" asked Chioma. "The concept I'm meaning."

"Well . . . it takes a certain type of unique pressure to produce diamonds, right? And my plan is to make my own spot the *diamond standard*, if y'all will, to have others model after it. This is to raise the standard from that of 'gold.' So, Tisha, you with Daddy on this one too, right? You know I need you."

"And you know I am, Daddy. Why would you even question that?"

"I don't. But good. Because I need you to rebuild the team to run the bar. I've already been busy gathering a team of bouncers together. And speaking of such, I so happened to have had a conversation with one of our guys from K.O.D.," Mitch mentioned.

"And that being who? Because it better not have been one of those negros that pledged their loyalty to that piece of crap, Ray-Ray, was it!?" Tisha stated.

"Actually, baby, it was with someone you were okay with."

"Who? The mixed boy, Adrian?"

"Nah. wasn't him."

"Well, who was it? Because I had a talk with someone myself who used to work security with the others," Tisha said.

Chioma's eyes roved from Mitch to Tisha, as the two exchanged inquiring words.

"With who? Because just like you said to me a moment ago, it better not had been with one of those niggaz that have pledged their loyalty to that piece of shit, Ray-Ray Stephens!" the father vented. Mitch managed to turn the point of focus from himself to Tisha now. "Who was it?" he urged Tisha to reveal.

"It was with Melvin, Daddy," she stated, "the last one to be hired to work security before Ray slimed you."

"Melvin? The quiet, suave type guy who stayed really clean and sharp?"

"Yep, him."

"And what he talking about? What's his intentions?" Mitch sought to know.

"To be honest, he's talking a lot. Really good stuff. And he's looking to get back into the business of security."

Chioma—like her sister—looked on at their father with a stern demeanor to await his reaction and reply to what Tisha made him aware of. She was already in the know of who it was that Tisha now dated. The big sister talked with her and no one else about all things personal and all things private. But how was their father to accept his daughter's choice of who she wanted to be intimate with? The moment was at hand to know.

"Tisha, how did you and Melvin manage to keep in contact with each other?" he asked with a smile of curiosity about his face.

"Daddy . . . he reached out to me through Yolanda. That's how we kept in touch," she said, technically lying so as to keep her father off her tail and all the way out of her business.

"Oh, that's how?"

"Yes, Daddy. That's how."

"And what's been up with Yolanda? I ain't seen or heard from her since that snake ass nigga, Ray-Ray, tore the K.O.D. family apart."

"She's been well, for the most part from what she said. She's investing her money wisely and trying her hand at a different location." Tisha lied to her father again to cover up the first lie.

"That's what's up. But yeah, text Melvin and let him know that I wouldn't mind welcoming him to a meeting with me to discuss a few things of importance to us both. Because, between us, I wanna see where his head is on everything, long before I just agree to do any level of business with him on my new team, since you seem to be vouching for him now. But I did tell you that I needed your help. And obviously, your referral of him is offering what you think may be helpful," Mitch stated.

"Exactly, Daddy! I'm glad to know you understand this," Tisha remarked.

"I get it, baby. I do. But like I said, I need to see where the boy's head is at. He *was* under Ray first, and I gotta be certain that dude ain't got nothing on him that rubbed off from him. Ray-Ray not right. He's a foul, toxic MF!"

"Gotcha. But I'll text him now to relay your message. Where would you like to meet?"

Chapter 17

Mitch took a pause before responding. He had a question for her about Melvin. "Does he even drink or smoke?"

"I don't really know, Daddy. He probably do."

"That'll be good if he does because, there's a new lowkey spot I wanna check out. It's called the *Maison F.P. Journe,* and is located inside the Kimpton hotel. There's an upscale bar that offers premium cigars and exclusive alcoholic drinks," Mitch said. "We can meet there."

"I believe I've read about this spot on the internet before. I've heard about it too. I can do a Google search for the address and send it to him if he's gonna agree to meet," Tisha responded.

TISHA: *Melvin, what's good, love! How are you? Hey, I had a talk with my dad today. He wants to meet with you about a job opportunity. He's got a new club exclusively owned by him. And now, he's busy going through the process to make everything legit. If you're willing to talk, he said he wants you to meet him at this new high-end bar. I'm about to forward the address to you now. It's inside the Kimpton hotel in South Beach, at the Maison F.P. Journe Bar.*

"What time, Daddy?" she asked.

"Tell him three o'clock would be good."

TISHA: *My dad says three is the time he'd like to meet with you today. Will you be available? And hopefully, the both of us could hook up later tonight. I wanna see you myself.*

Moments later, Melvin replied.

MELVIN: *Hey, Tisha! I'm well, sweetie. Thanks for asking. And yes, I'm willing to meet with your Pops today. I wouldn't mind having a business conversation with him, by the way. Today at three is good. And the spot he wants to link up, the Maison F.P. Journe Bar inside the Kimpton hotel, is cool. The name sounds exotic and reads like it's high value. A top dollar spot. Lol!*

Melvin also became curious to know what it was about this high-end spot in particular that made Mitch want to meet him there.

TISHA: *LMAO! Baby, you should already know by now that my daddy loves the finer things that life has to offer. He's the reason why I'm the way I am, boo. High maintenance as fuck! But I'll hit you up later, my love. Daddy speaking to me again, and I don't want him asking too many questions about my smiles to your words, about my reactions to your replies, or about our extended communication, okay? But I'm about to forward you the address. Just Google the directions and use your GPS. Much love! xoxoxo*

MELVIN: *Much love to you as well. Xoxo*

Tisha turned her attention back to her father. "Daddy, Melvin said that he'll be there at three for sure to meet you."

"Okay. That's what's up. But on another note, Chioma, if you don't mind, baby, could you please let your daddy and your sister talk for a moment?" Mitch requested of his youngest daughter.

"No problem, Daddy. I understand," she responded, got to her feet, and made her way from the living room to the kids' domains. She went to Bella's first.

Mitch then proceeded with Tisha in private now. "Look, baby. Here in the bag I got with me, is $300,000 to go with what you're already holding for me. How much, with this, does it make in all?"

"Hmm . . . let me see. I'm holding $700,000, plus the $300K here. That's a million total. Then there's $400K worth in those silver ingots," Tisha responded in a whisper to her father.

"That sounds about right, baby. And more than likely, by the end of next week, I'll be dropping off maybe another $300,000, okay? Your cousin, Roland, is taking care of things for me, and it's paying off. Also," he said then dug into the pocket of his pants and pulled out a thick bankroll, "here. Take this and do something nice for the kids." Mitch peeled off $4,000. "Now Daddy gotta go for now. Me and your stepmother to be, Olivia, going out to dinner later today once my meeting with Melvin is complete. And I want you to know you're doing a really good job with running the business of yours we got up and going. These entities are washing the money well. We're able to keep the IRS off our asses too by being sure to pay Uncle Sam. I'm planning a future trip to Haiti for us. It won't be one so soon but soon enough though. I gotta go over there to know exactly how the family's compound we're having built is coming along. That goddamn earthquake back then, managed to destroy so much. I also gotta do what I can to help a few of our family members there get visas and have access here to the States, because when I finally open the doors to Club Pressure, I want everything to be A-one. I'm pretty sure there'll be a few haters somewhere in the mix, who's gonna be comin' at me in a way like never before. And I've got to see your grandmother over in Haiti, to get the spiritual protection I need. Momma's gotta hook me up. I need it. But anyways, y'all take care, baby, and Daddy loves you," Mitch stated without exhaustion, then got to his feet, kissed Tisha on the forehead, then exited the home.

Tisha took the bag of money and made her way to the brick structure wash house that was situated in her backyard. A safe was installed in the wall of the place. The level of trust and reliability that her father had in her regarding the safekeeping of his money and other valuable possessions, said a lot about how confident he was in her and her decision-making skills. However, Tisha had a love interest in her life now, and so, special attention needed to be paid to him and the idea he may have in mind.

This was subject to complicate things with the father.

Chapter 18

Later in the day, Mitch found himself seated inside the Maison F.P. Journe bar, patiently awaiting Melvin to arrive. He passed the time sipping on a cocktail and puffing on a premium cigar, a La Palina Black Label Robusto. The street boss he thought himself as, really begin feeling good and self-assured. His level of articulation was thorough as could be, as he spit his game and popped flavor to the pretty young tender of his he'd brought along to accompany the occasion. Her name was Valerie. He was nearly thirty years her senior. Mitch also was sure to tip the bartender handsomely for the quality service provided. It was a Spanish guy named Ramos.

"Sir, would you like to try one of our rare and unusual liquors from Russia that we offer?" asked Ramos of Mitch.

"Most certainly, I would. What you got? Because me personally, I love Russian spy novels. I love Russian oligarchs form of government. And I love the Russian Mafia. In addition, I greatly admire Vladimir Putin and the Kremlin. So, what is it that you got to offer, that came from Russia . . . with love, maybe?" Mitch replied. He checked the time on his Ulysse Nardin and envisioned himself in a way as a wealthy Russian sailor, paralleling the nautical timepiece.

Ramos spoke again. "Well, sir, we have an exclusive Soviet-Era Moskovskaya Vodka that I can draw from the cellar of ours, where we keep the rare stuff, and pour you up a few shots," he stated.

"Well . . . we do have a designated driver on hand, just in case I get to feeling myself a little too much and down more drinks than I should be doing, while out in public." Mitch was referring to his personal bodyguard/driver who was also there. He and Valerie raised their glasses and toasted to the words that proceeded from his mouth.

Mitch had the appearance of a nightlife promoter, or that of a high-profile music mogul. His hair was cut low in an all-around Caesar temp-fade, and his beard had a razor-sharp line-up about it, as it was thick, dark, and full, well connected to the moustache. "How much for each shot?" Mitch asked.

"They'll cost you four hundred bucks a glass, sir," Ramos replied.

"Well . . . start pouring 'em up, my guy. Four hundred a shot is not a problem for Mitchell Duvalier-Collins. Hell . . . if this *rare* stuff you seem to speak so fond of, is as good as you make it out to be, I may have my own bartenders serving it up in Club Pressure that's set to open soon," stated Mitch in a confident tone of voice.

Ramos departed to go fetch a bottle of the throwback liquor Mitch agreed to spend money on. Moments later, he was back in the presence of the client. "Here you are, sir," he professed. "The speciality you requested." Two thick shot glasses were placed on the counter. Ramos began to fill each.

Mitch took one and turned it up. The powerful liquor cleared any and all forms of congestion he had. "Damn! This some strong stuff here! Woo!!! It got some kick to it too! My-my!" he declared. It took him maybe three minutes to kill the first shot. He and Valerie downed the other together. The glasses were two and a half inches tall. Ramos began to pour up another.

At this time, Melvin was pulling up to the building. The valet was positioned to take the car and park it for him. He stepped from the driver's seat draped from head to toe in a stylish suit with a bow tie. Ascot Chang was the designer and label's name. On Melvin's feet were a pair of fabulous

Fratelli Rossetti loafers to accentuate the suit. The watch was a stainless steel Rotonde de Cartier, a welcome home gift to him by his cousin, Vick, along with the threads and the shoes. Vick was the type of leader and business minded guy that wanted everyone on his team to wear expensive suits and merchandise to any and all meetings he was to host, and likewise, for them to any and all subsequent meetings they were to appear at outside of his. The intention was to instil a professional mindset into his people and establish a captivating culture of the group.

Chapter 19

Melvin stepped through the front door of the hotel and made his way to the bar that was visible behind a large thick glass wall. He roved his head in awe at the sheer opulence put upon display of the hotel's interior. The luxurious chandelier that was above his figure had to have cost a million dollars or more. In continuing forward, Melvin strutted one then two steps toward Mitch's direction at the sight of him seated at the counter of the bar.

He took notice of a female and a lean-fit dude by Mitch's side. It was immediately presumed by Melvin that the youthful looking lady and the gentlemen present, were a girlfriend and a bodyguard. Upon Melvin getting at a distance of about fifteen feet from the host of the meeting, he was approached by the protector. There were orders prescribed beforehand for the security personnel to cut down any and every one in a pat search for weapons before they were to have access to Mitch. Melvin respected the assignment. He spread his arms wide to be frisked. There were no ill feelings about this.

"Nothing personal, my guy. It's strictly business. Strictly business, fam. That's it," said the bodyguard to Melvin throughout the process.

"Not a problem. I understand," Melvin responded.

Once the check was complete, Melvin walked up to Mitch to shake his hand. The two embraced as well. They took a seat, and the conversation began.

"How you been, Melvin? It's nice to see you again. I'm glad to have you meet me here," stated Mitch.

"As always, I've been well, Mitchell-Mitch," he responded in a witty way. "And it's an honor to have you invite me to this meeting with you. I feel privileged in a way," Melvin further said, roving his eyes and head once more in awe at the place. "And what's that you drinking on there, bro? That 'ish looks like it belongs to royalty!"

"Oh, this right here?" Mitch answered up then pointed to the glass of rare Russian vodka. The bartender had the exquisitely shaped and designed bottle in their presence as well. He smiled at the compliment made by Melvin.

Mitch continued with the boastful remark he was intent on making. "Boy, this 'ish right here, running me four hundred a shot, bro. It's some rare and unusual Soviet-era Russian vodka. Ain't that's how you termed it, Ramos Rozay, aka Double R?" He'd given the bartender a nickname that quick.

"Yes, Mr. Collins. That's how it's termed . . . rare and unusual," replied Ramos.

"And by the way, how do you like the new nickname that I gave you?" Mitch teased.

"It's fine by me, Mr. Collins."

"Perfect! Because from this day forward, every time I come back to visit this place, that's the name I'm gonna call you by . . . either Ramos Rozay or Double R," Mitch declared. Valerie giggled in delight at tipsy Mitch. "But anyway, what would you like to drink, Melvin? That's if you do so?" He pointed at the many choices there were to choose from.

"Hmm . . . let me see. I wouldn't mind tasting that Pappy Van Winkle twenty-year-old family Reserved there." He pointed to the bottle that had an elder man on it puffing on a long, expensive looking cigar. "Damn! This is a high-end cigar bar too, I see," he acknowledged. Melvin appeared to be mesmerized.

"Now, Melvin, you should already know by now that ol' Mitch here, only aim for and strive to have nothing but the best. Absolutely an exquisite cigar bar to go along with the liquor. So, drink and smoke up. It's all on me, Mitch—the real boss I know myself to be," he said to his guest with much enthusiasm.

"Dope. Very dope," Melvin responded. "Double R, let me puff on one of those Tatuaje Jekyll joints you got there." He pointed while requesting.

"Absolutely, sir. And you are?" Ramos inquired.

"I'm Melvin. But everyone calls me Parlay, because that's what I love to do—lay back, kick it, and chill. Just like we're doing now. But whichever name you prefer to address me by is cool with me." He then turned to acknowledge the young lady who was present. "My apologies, ma'am. I didn't mean to be rude. I was intent on greeting you but was momentarily sidetracked. As you may have heard by now, I'm Melvin. Nice to meet you," he properly introduced himself then extended a hand to shake hers.

"I'm Valerie. Nice to meet you as well," she replied. The two shook hands. Melvin then turned back toward Mitch to discuss the business at hand.

"So, Mitch, what you got in mind to discuss? I'm here. What the business is, my guy?!"

"What the business be is this. I'm *back* in business, Melvin. And this time around, I'm all by my lonely in ownership. Won't no slime ass nigga be able to snake me again. I'm gonna assure myself of that," Mitch declared in a strong, confident way.

"Is that right?"

"No doubt."

"That's what's up though. I'm feeling you on that," Melvin let out, hit his drink, and took a toke of the tobacco. "Back in business, you say, as in the clubbing business, right?" Melvin didn't really have in-depth knowledge of the rift that occurred between Mitch and Mr. Raymond. He'd only heard bits and pieces. However, never anything directly from either of the two.

"Of course, playboy. Back in the clubbing business."

"Where?"

"The building that used to be the old Club Ice. That spot," Mitch informed.

"Oh. That one. I'm more than sure you've got a few renovations to have done on that spot before you open the doors to it, don't you?" It was obvious to anyone who laid eyes on the building that it could use some work.

"Everything already in progress, my guy. I'm gonna give it a new name and all."

"You are?"

"For sho."

"To what?"

"Club Pressure."

"Club Pressure, huh? That's a catchy name for a club. If I heard of something new to party at with that name, hell, I'd wanna see what it's talking about myself," Melvin said.

"I know, right?" Mitch responded. "But anyway, look. The main reason I invited you to meet me today was because, I'm looking to build a team of bona fide bouncers to be security over the new spot. And it's all the better, if I can get the majority of the old family to join me for the ride. At least I know I can trust the ones I'm hand-picking, the guys who I brought along before. I got Bo Jack onboard, also Roc, Dey-Dey, G-Dep, AP, Peeco, and, I'm hoping I can convince you to get down with us."

Chapter 20

Melvin took a pause to think over all Mitch had propositioned to him. He then had a question or two for the host of their meeting. "So, how many days a week you looking to have the security working?"

"Three to four to begin with. And as we progress, we'll move on up like that," explained Mitch.

"And where would I fit into the equation, if I decided to tag along?"

"Well . . . you should already know that I gotta have Bo Jack leading the way, due to how much experience he has over everybody else, and also, on the strength of how familiar I am with him. But, I can have you at second in command as his right-hand to lead the pack at any time he's not available. Because I believe that eventually, I'm gonna be pushed to move you on up to the top spot in one way or another."

"Damn! Why you say it like that, Mitch? 'Eventually, you're gonna be pushed to move me on up to the top spot in one way or another?'"

"Nigga! Don't try to play mind games with me. I ain't no goddamn fool! A man knows any daughters of his well enough. And it's not rocket science to figure out that my daughter, Tisha, got the hots for you, boy. I've seen the faces she makes at any time your name is brought up. And, I can't help but to know what the smiles of hers be all about that comes along with those expressions she displays. So, y'all two ain't got nothing going on that I don't readily observe," Mitch stated. He had a smirk about his face as he looked on at Melvin.

Melvin snickered and made a smile behind the words of Mitch. He had to turn his head away from him in an attempt to try and hide the guilt he was called out on. "We're just cool, Mitch. That's about it. Tisha respects the way that I articulate to her and provide advice. Simply put, we're good friends. Nothing more." He'd told Mitch a bold-faced lie right there direct and personally. But Mitch seemed to take it all in.

"Yeah, yeah, yeah. Good friends and nothing more, my ass! The bottom line is, I don't really give a shit, Melvin. But . . . I'm gonna tell you straight up, playboy. My daughter is a grown woman with two kids. I don't run her life, nor do I try to. She does. Tisha is free to see whoever she chooses to see and do whatever she chooses to do, with whoever she's seeing. However, if my daughter comes to me **ONE TIME**, about some foul shit that you've done to her, or on her with some other female . . . then, there's gonna be a major problem between you and me, my nigga! Are we understood on that?!" Mitch had a finger pointed in Melvin's face as he made his declaration to him. The gesture to Melvin was only to let him know that he was so for real about his daughter. Nothing more.

Melvin appeared to comprehend the meaning of the message conveyed to him. He took notice that Mitch really didn't have a problem with now knowing he was involved with his daughter. A bit of a confession was put out there by him. "You don't ever have to worry about that occurring, Mitch. I'm not that type of dude."

"I don't really give a shit! Just continue to do what you do. But be a man about *all* that you do. And don't make no excuses. Other than that, I like you, Melvin. I get a good vibe and all from you, my guy. Hell, if I didn't know any better, I probably would begin to think that you were busy trying to outdo me in dressing, with those sharp-ass threads you got on there, along with those shoes," Mitch let out. He then brushed the shoulders of Melvin and popped the collar of his shirt. "So, what you say . . . you in? You with me?"

Melvin paused yet again in such a moment to think over all that the two of them had discussed. He then gave an answer. "Yeah, Mitch. I'm in. I'm with you, bro. Go on ahead and put me down as a team player. But I'm gonna work only three days out the week, because that's all I'm able to do. At least for right now," he responded.

"Bet. Thursday, Fridays, and Saturdays. I got you on that. I'm glad to know we've made progress with this meeting here. It's official. Club Pressure, the gentlemen's night lounge, is subject to be the most happening spot in all of Miami. My plan is to outperform everything that King of Dimez had going on."

Mitch stood to his feet and proclaimed this message to the eight or so patrons on hand that listened and who'd visited the bar. He then raised his glass above his head in a triumphant manner as if to claim victory. A slight stagger occurred in the process. The effects of the shots he'd downed had him tipsy. For certain, it had to have been the "rare and unusual" Russian vodka that had him in the chill zone. Or it could've been the pre-embargo Cuban rum he'd sampled as well. Either or, the statement he'd made about the new spot outperforming K.O.D., Melvin thought that to be a remark a bit farfetched. Absurd even. Pure smoke being blown. A threat of wishful thinking on Mitch's behalf. A pipedream even.

The two continued to discuss things and had a few more rounds of cocktails prior to exchanging contact information and giving word to keep in touch.

"Mitch, you be sure to get at me when the doors open to the new joint. And I thank you too, bro, for offering the opportunity," Melvin said.

"I plan to definitely do that, my guy. And you only need to be sure that you take things easy on the heart of my daughter, nigga! That's all you need to be concerned with!" responded Mitch. He pointed his finger at Melvin once more to imply how serious he was about Tisha. He was so for real.

Melvin laughed it off as a playful thing, shook his hand, then tore it down in fast stepping, and headed out the door on his way to a seminar related to business and account management. He was seeking to enhance his knowledge in the world of finances. Overall, the meeting proved to be a success.

Chapter 21

Following the flight across the Gulf of Mexico made by the delegated group of persons led by Mr. Raymond, the plane landed in Cancun, one of the most popular tourist destinations in all the world. To accompany Mr. Raymond, there was the nephew, Phillip Jr., Phillip Jr.'s girlfriend, Ericka, the mistress of Mr. Raymond, Felicia, and the lone most trusted bodyguard of his who he believed in as though he believed in Christ the Messiah as a Savior, Willie.

Mr. Raymond and the nephew had a high stakes meeting to be present for with the cartel leader who supplied them. His name was Mr. Ramirez Chucho. The duty was for the nephew to be confirmed by Mr. Ramirez, to be the successor to the uncle whenever the time was to come. Also, Phillip Jr. was required to be initiated into the brotherhood order that the elder two were a part of. This was to be done directly by the cartel chieftain himself. Phillip Jr. wouldn't receive not one brick of product until he was to do so.

Mr. Ramirez sent a team of men to the city limit to pick up Mr. Raymond and Phillip Jr. only. The others would remain behind at the resort and allowed the opportunity to partake of the pleasantries the vacation afforded. The uncle and nephew were in for a three-hour drive inland for the clandestine meeting at the compound of Mr. Ramirez. The site was walled off with a barbwire and razor-wired topping to keep out would-be intruders. In addition, the area was thoroughly equipped with a litany of surveillance cameras all about the entirety of the locale to keep watch for the authorities trying to raid or other rival cartels attempting to take Mr. Ramirez out the game. On a permanent basis.

Once arriving to the compound, Mr. Raymond and Phillip Jr. were then escorted poolside of the mansion where Mr. Ramirez was situated. He stood to his feet to greet his American guests. They all shook hands—he to them and them to he.

"Hello! And welcome, gentlemen. As always, it's a pleasure to meet with you again, Raymond. I'm hoping that the flight was well for you two," said Mr. Ramirez with a smile. He displayed the silver crowned teeth of his. They covered the pre-molars on both sides.

"My pleasure as well, Señor. How do you do?" Mr. Raymond responded. "This here is my nephew, Señor, the one I mentioned to you before." Mr. Raymond put a hand in the small of Phillip Jr.'s back to urge him to step closer.

The nephew smiled and nodded his head. "It's a privilege to meet you, Señor. I couldn't hardly wait to be in this moment. And now, it's finally here," Phillip Jr. said to the cartel drug lord.

"So, you're the one who Raymond has assured me shall be the dutiful distributor for the Chucho family in the U.S. too, huh?" said Mr. Ramirez in the broken English he spoke. Although not fluent, his understanding of the language was sufficient to speak it and know exactly what was said to him in an American tongue.

"Oh, yes, I am the one to lead my family and the enterprise that we have functioning, all by the blessings of you, sir, and my uncle here," Phil Jr. responded.

"Please . . . I'd like to go ahead and begin the process, if you two will," Mr. Ramirez stated, then led the way toward a little guest house that was connected to the pool house.

Although the guests had just journeyed on a three-hour trip from the beach side resort to the residence of Mr. Ramirez, they had no time to rest. The process was set to begin. Not to mention, the weather was hot and dry for the day. The building that they entered was furnished with air conditioning.

They entered. The inside was a bit cozy and pleasing to the eyes. There was a thick, fluffy carpet all throughout, a kitchenette, a decent bathroom, and a dining section. There was a circular, dark cherry oak wood table that seated seven. Mr. Ramirez directed that they all take a chair and situate themselves. Those present were to also include the underboss of Mr. Ramirez, the top general of his security forces, a translator to ensure everything was communicated properly, and a male servant to perform specific chores and catering.

The energy and the vibe within the conclave was positive and business orientated. "Pedro," Mr. Ramirez called out to the servant. "Please put on music and get me and my guests drinks," he related in English, wanting not to offend his non-Spanish speaking visitors. He wished not to cause them to feel uncomfortable or disrespected.

"What would you two like to drink?" Mr. Ramirez asked of the uncle and nephew.

"Hey! You know me, Señor," responded Mr. Raymond first. "Each time I have the opportunity to come say hello in person, I always ask for tequila. Besides, I'm in Mexico. I must enjoy the popular drink," he further said with a smile. "And my nephew here, he likes what I like. He'll have the same."

Chapter 22

Mr. Ramirez returned a smile of his own behind the reply Mr. Raymond made. "I have exclusive cigars as well, Raymond. I know you love to smoke those along with your drink. You and me both are similar," he stated. The attention then went to the servant. "Pedro, could you please provide my guests the top shelf drinks they've asked for and a box of cigars? Be sure to bring their gifts I have for them also," he instructed.

The servant jumped to the occasion and moved with efficiency at the orders given by the boss. Mr. Ramirez turned back to Mr. Raymond and Phil Jr. once more. He called the meeting to full order at that point. "Raymond, you're having no problems on your end, I assume, with getting the goods into your possession that I send, are you?"

"No, sir, Señor. All is well. Everything is running smoothly with our operation. Like a well-oiled machine."

"So, the well-crafted coffin disguise and the ceramic sculpture pieces arrive timely and non-tampered with?"

"Yes, sir, they do. I like the way we've been doing business in this particular manner. It's working out well the way we're going about this, as I'm supplied only three times yearly. Low risk for me and my brother, Emanuel, the old man! And we reap great rewards," responded Mr. Raymond.

"Ah, yes . . . Emanuel. 'The old man!' How's he?"

"He's well. Always moving and keeping busy. He's very determined to live past a hundred," Mr. Raymond let out with a slight chuckle.

"I remember him well. He used to make me feel old," remarked Mr. Ramirez. He'd met Emanuel on a few occasions on his trips to the States and at any time Emanuel accompanied Mr. Raymond on a trip to Mexico.

"Yes, Emanuel. He taught me everything I know. At least from the point of my brother departing us physically to where I'm at now in this line of business. But Emanuel, is the one who keeps the product tucked away securely. He asked me to tell you hello for him and that he'll be able to return here to visit with us on the next trip. But as you know, my nephew, Phil Jr. here, shall be my face and voice to report to our mandatory meetings three times yearly."

Chapter 23

Mr. Ramirez turned to speak directly to Phil Jr. now. "Phillip . . . you are aware that your uncle here has left big shoes for you to fill, correct?" he asked.

"I'm very aware, Mr. Chucho." He referred to him in a more formal fashion by addressing him by his surname. The host smiled at the gesture. "My uncle was sure to thoroughly groom me to take over and lead our family in this regard, the same as he had. But his attention is elsewhere now to proceed, to live out the dream my grandfather held for him, and, that of his own personal ambitions, which is to lead our city," the young one stated to Mr. Chucho.

"So I've been told," Mr. Chucho commented then changed the subject. "Let's get started before the pleasantries are served, shall we?"

Everyone followed the lead of Mr. Chucho by getting to their feet and walking over to an adjoining room. The flooring to it was thick and plush with carpeting. There were dark colored padded walls, an elegant chandelier directly situated above the center of the room, and a gold-colored circular tile section below the chandelier. There sat a three-step podium in front of the dais. It was three feet wide and three feet long. Three cushioned seats sat behind the podium.

Mr. Chucho's three men to accompany him sat in the chairs behind him at the podium while Mr. Raymond and Phil Jr. occupied the bench that sat before him.

"Session is now in," Mr. Chucho declared.

Everyone already had their shirts tucked inside their pants and began to remove their shoes. Mr. Raymond previously made known to Phil Jr. all that was to take place; that way, he wouldn't be lost on the formalities of the process.

"Nephew, listen," Mr. Raymond whispered to Phil Jr. like an elder would to a youth while in church. "The moment that you see Señor step up on the podium, I'm gonna need for you to go and stand directly in the middle of that circle there, put your feet together, cross your hand left over right at your belt buckle, and pay close attention to all that he says, okay? This is the part I told you about; the initiation process. Your big day. Nothing will be the same for you from here onward," informed Mr. Raymond.

Mr. Chucho took to the podium. Little Phil did as instructed. Suddenly, the lights went dim. The only beam to continue shining was the one from the chandelier above Phil Jr.'s head. Mr. Chucho began to recite his ceremonial preamble that was to last every bit of five minutes. He spoke in Spanish first then translated to the best he could in English.

Chapter 24

In The Meantime...

Back at the hotel resort in Cancun, Willie was entrusted to stand guard over Felicia and Erica until Mr. Raymond and Phil Jr. returned. One part of Willie's duties was easy to fulfil; that related to Erica. She'd drank entirely too much upon stepping foot on Mexican soil and found herself sick as a stray dog and laid up in the suite. Felicia, always curious to dig deeper into the business of Mr. Raymond, made it a priority to call Willie on the phone, to have a conversation with him regarding her benefactor. Who better to know the most about Mr. Raymond other than the man who got paid to protect him?

Willie entered the room and took a seat as asked of him. "How old are you, Willie?" Felicia didn't beat around the bush with what she wanted to know. Willie posed a smirk then proceeded with a reply.

"What makes you think that I'm *old,* per se?" he put it back to her by answering a question with a question. It was a playful banter to say the least.

"Well, I didn't mean *old* in that sense. Let me rephrase it then. What's your age? How's that?" she corrected with a smile.

"That's better. But if you must know, I'm forty-seven, Lisa." He referred to her in the short version of her name.

"You're forty-seven, huh? You look fairly young."

"You don't say. After you just told me that I was old," he joked in his quick witty reply. Felicia smiled at the acute wits Willie displayed.

"You're in good shape. What's the secret? How do you maintain that youthful physique, the features, and the healthy skin you possess?" she asked.

"For me, proper exercise. Vegan diet. Plenty of water. And a young tender to keep me sexually pleased. Those are the keys to my success," Willie related.

"*Hmm.* That sounds very interesting. And didn't I hear you say, vegan?"

"You did. I'm an earth-centered person. I tend to practice being a conscious-minded man. And I find that my true wealth is that of having good health. A vegan diet is the cleanest and best diet of them all. Therefore, I consume no flesh. Anything with a face or from animal origin, I don't do," Willie stated.

"Ah, man . . . I believe I'd die if I couldn't eat meat. I gotta have it. But anyway, how long you and Ray been good friends?" Felicia asked.

"Ray and I been cool many years now. About thirty-five years to be exact. At least that's how long I've been knowing him. He and an uncle of mine grew up together. He's doing life in federal prison. Been down now for twenty-two years."

"Oh, wow! He's been locked up almost as long as I've been living. You got any kids, Willie?"

"I do. I got two sons. One's your age, and the other's twenty-three," he replied.

"How you know my age, Willie?" Felicia asked with a humorous giggle.

"I know all that's needed to be known about you, young lady."

"Oh! *You* don't say."

"That's right. You should know that if I'm the man's bodyguard, he has to tell me everything he's got going on. I have to do details for Christine, Erin, and also Ray Jr., at any time he comes home to visit.

"Oh, Ray's got a son?!" Felicia asked. She was taken by surprise at the revelation.

"Of course he does. The boy's the brain behind the family's businesses in a way. The nigga is smart as shit! He graduated from Dartmouth College. The father and son are cool now. But for a long time, they didn't get along. Ray put him out at an early age. He went to live with the aunt, Ray's sister. She's the one who raised him," Willie related.

"I guess it ain't my two cents to know why they didn't get along. But Ray never mentioned him to me. Is Christine the mother?"

"Nah. His mother's name is Mildred . . . Mildred Askews. Ray took custody of the son when he was three and sent him to live with the aunt when he was twelve."

Felicia switched up the conversation to something more related to her. "Willie, look, at times, I be having a guilty conscious about my being involved with Ray. Does his wife know about us?" she asked with a serious tone.

"It's not so much about her knowing about you, per se, that matters. She's aware of the type of lifestyle that Ray enjoys, and has no problem with it. Why? Because she doesn't see anything. And it would be different if he took it upon himself to rub it in her face, as if to say *fuck you!* But he does no such thing. I have to give him much respect for being a man in that sense. He's very respectful in that regard. They've been through a lot together. Her position is simple. As long as Ray does right by her, he can do all he so pleases. That four-million-dollar house they live in, it's in her name. Also, she has a couple of businesses of her own and a few real estate properties. So, don't concern yourself too much worrying about Christine. She's good. You just need to figure out how to secure yourself in his life in that way. Because you're very important to him, Lisa. Probably more than you know. That's the only reason I said all I did to you about his personal life. The man loves you. And you're not gonna fuck that up or play on his feelings and emotions either!" He smiled at her. This was followed by a slight chuckle.

"So, Ray loves me?"

"The man really loves you and believes in you, Lisa. He tells me all the time that he plans on continuing to take care of you, and eventually, elevating you to a high level to be a woman of power and prestige. That way, once he gets too old to carry on, or if Christine divorces and leaves, you'll be there to hold him down. You'll be the one to remain by his side. He's gonna put you over the money," stated Willie. He provided Felicia with revelation after revelation. things she had no knowledge about.

"Is that right, Willie? I'm glad to know that. But yeah, I'm aware that he likes me a lot. This is our second vacation together. And he can't seem to get enough of me. Ray bought me a brand-new car. He moved me and my kids into a bigger house—one he owns. And, I can't get enough of him, let alone, thank him enough. My son, Jeremiah, loves and appreciates Ray more than he does his own dad. And my daughter, Drea, adores the man as well. But what about you, Willie? Ray's got a wife and a mistress in me. What's your personal life like, playboy?" Felicia's nosey ass questioned on and on.

Chapter 25

Although Willie wasn't in the habit of revealing his personal life to anyone, let alone a random fling to the man he worked for, he took it upon himself to entertain the occasion by doing so. "Now, Lisa, use your common sense for a moment if you will. I'm the personal bodyguard to the man who once owned the hottest strip club that there has ever been in America. You should know that I had to have enjoyed my fair share of the females who passed through. I was surrounded by too many to not do so. But no. I don't have a wife. I've never been married. I'm too promiscuous for that type of lifestyle. And I love variety. I love choices. I like having options when it comes to women. However, I do have a girlfriend. We've been together now three years. Our chemistry is great. We're very compatible because we both enjoy the simple pleasures of life. Neither one of us are hard to please. It doesn't take much to keep her happy. That's the part I like," Willie related to her. Felicia appeared to be enthralled at his honest peep into his life.

"So, what's her age, if you don't mind me asking?" Felicia continued. "I'm sure she may be a young love interest like me," she let out with a smile. Willie returned one of his own.

"She's twenty-nine."

"See, I knew it," she smiled. "A young sweetheart like I am."

"That's right. Only a few years older than you. A man has to always keep a young lady around. Y'all are the ones responsible for keeping us relevant. The more energy and vigor we have, the longer that we live," admitted Willie.

"That's understandable. I've never heard it in that way before. And what's the girlfriend's name?"

"Her name is Shunika. We call her Nika for short."

"Will the two of us ever meet?"

"You may in due time."

"Well, good. And I'm sure that Nika, truly appreciates the suave, savvy, and handsome guy that you are, Willie. It's evident that you and Ray have been friends for quite some time now. A lot of him has rubbed off on you. In all the good ways. Look at you. You're physically fit. You eat properly and clean. Your skin, nails, and hair is of good health. You're smart and speak well. And, you have a nice style and flavor about yourself. There's no doubt. You should manage to go a long way in love and relationship," Felicia complimented. She admired Willie in a major way. Her eyes, energy, and body language said it all.

"Well, I thank you, Lisa. I really do. Your kind words goes a long way with me," he expressed graciously.

A thought came to Felicia's mind. It was something that Willie mentioned that she wanted to go back over once more. "Look, you brought up the fact that Ray's wife may be looking to file for divorce at some point. I want to know how is she? And why is divorce in the equation?" Felicia inquired.

"Well, that's just the way Ray feels and thinks about their marriage. I do know that he's slowly fading from her though," Willie responded.

"Why you say that?"

"It speaks for itself. They barely do anything together anymore. Not to mention the fact that she's in her mid-fifties. So, I'm sure you may know that the sex life isn't there no more. That's obvious."

"I know, right?" Felicia quickly injected and let out with a chuckle and a smile.

"If anybody, I'm sure you're aware of that more so than not. But they're alright with each other. Not happy. Ray's remedy with how he deals with her is simple. Just give her what she asks for. He doesn't do anything in her face to disrespect the marriage. And he sends her on expensive gambling and shopping trips when she wants to go—she and her best friend, Zandra. His responsibility to her is easy," Willie related.

"And by you acting as security for her as well, I'm sure that the both of you have carried on deep progressive conversations as well, the same like we are doing now, huh?"

"Indeed, we have. Christine is not like you though. She doesn't know how to have a sensible conversation without trying to get me to speak on all the things Ray's got going on outside of their marriage. She's aware that I'm exposed to a lot and knows I won't speak on nothing when it comes to what *my boss* does or has going on. She needs to hire a private detective for that. Not me. I could get fired or worse, lose my life behind yapping at the mouth too much. That's what—pardon my language—bitches and gay niggaz do! I'm too real for that type of shit. I've let Ray know many times about the actions and demands made to me by the wife. He limited the hours that I was to hold detail over her to prevent this — as to allow it space to die down. The pressing of me for information didn't really start until the two week long trip he and you were away on in Turks and Caicos."

"That was not long after he sold the club."

"Exactly. But, if you must know, there's a reason why I told you all that I have. You'll know soon enough. I've said a mouthful already. And it's funny because of all the years I've known Ray and been security for the man and the female companions he's been involved with, they've never gotten me to talk to them as much as you have with you. But like I said . . . all of this has a purpose and a meaning to it. So don't take it for granted," Willie stated.

"Don't worry. I won't," Felicia replied.

"I just know how the man thinks and feels about you. And eventually, I'll be security for you from time to time as you continue to grow and mature and morph into the type of lady that Ray has plans for you to be, Lisa. The nigga has a good chance to be the mayor of Miami. He has plans to have you educated and trained to be his top secretary. You'll have huge responsibilities in due time, little lady. So, you may as well continue to make yourself comfortable with me."

"You right about that, Willie," Felicia responded. A dash of anxiety appeared across her face after being made aware of the expectations Mr. Raymond would soon have of her and the fear she held of failing to live up to that standard.

"But anyway, let's drink up on the wine and champagne they have for us to choose from on this menu here. I think I'll have a bottle of the Stones and Bones 2015. I sampled it before. Good stuff," Willie said. They continued to become acquainted with one another and carry on graciously as a protector and the protected should.

Chapter 26

Back at the compound of the cartel leader, Mr. Ramirez Chucho, he'd completed the preamble portion of the initiation and approached Phil Jr. to complete the process.

"From this point forward," Mr. Chucho said with a hand on the shoulder of the young kingpin in the making, "all I need for you to pronounce is either I do or I don't to the questions I'm going to ask of you. Understood?"

"Yes, Señor. I understand," the pupil replied.

"Good. Now, by you providing your oath and by you being initiated into the order that we have, do you fully understand that absolutely nothing comes before this. . . the order?" asked Mr. Chucho.

"I do," Phil Jr. responded.

"And when we say *nothing*, we mean *nothing*; Not God . . . not wife . . . not kids . . . not parents . . . not family . . . not otherwise . . . comes before this order?" Mr. Chucho stated in an emphatic manner. "Do you understand?"

"I do."

"You do know that your life, the life of your family, the life of your kids, and the life of anyone you love dearly, is on the line by any failure on your part that you're unable to correct?"

"I do."

"Do you hereby swear to faithfully and dutifully surrender your life, your soul, and all of you spiritually, to this order that you now wish to be a member of?"

"I do."

"Do you—Phillip LeRon Stephens the second—swear before the God of the heavens above, to uphold, honor, and worship the constitution that governs this order; the oath that you have professed, and the wisdom that you possess to propel you forward and that strengthens the ranks of this glorious society that we have here?"

"I do."

Mr. Chucho then withdrew a sharp, two-inch razor blade from his pocket, grabbed hold of Phil Jr.'s left hand, cut a puncture wound in the thumb to produce a droplet of blood; allowed it to drip onto an index card sized picture of a saint draped in a cassock and other formal accentuates and absorb, then proceeded with the final phase of the ceremony.

"And lastly, do you completely understand that if you are to ever betray this order that you have just been made a part of, you shall surely die and burn in hell as the ones who suffered the same consequences?" Mr. Chucho asked.

"I do," Phil Jr. emphatically responded.

Phil was then given a paper towel to clean his thumb, peroxide, tape, and a small tube of antibacterial cream to treat himself. Mr. Chucho grabbed Phil Jr. by the head gently with both hands and pulled him lower. He kissed the newly made man on the forehead.

"Congratulations, my fellow brethren. Welcome to the order that we have established," Mr. Chucho declared. "By the power and authority invested within me, you are officially part of the family."

Mr. Raymond stood to his feet and walked over to congratulate as well. So did Mr. Chucho's other men who were present. Phil Jr. was hugged and kissed by the uncle too. "You made it, nephew. You've now officially taken my place. I'm out the way," he said to him. Phil Jr. was all smiles and delighted to know he was finally a boss.

They all exited the door of the small lodge and made their way to the dining room of the mansion. The servants had prepared the table with pastries, top quality boxes of cigars, champagne, wine, and liquor. And then, in walked five beautiful Mexican models to please and delight the gentlemen on the special occasion. Classical music began to play.

"Remember, Phil, there is no way out," Mr. Chucho whispered into his ear on the subject one last time. He then departed the area, leaving the guests to enjoy themselves with the lovely Senoritas.

Phil Jr. was in a new world now, one where there was little room for error and severe punishment behind any mishap.

Chapter 27

Mitch was sure to take proactive steps to exercise the ambition he possessed to make his new night spot, Club Pressure, a favorite party destination and playboy lounge for those who valued and appreciated this type of socialization. He'd also taken a backseat in a way from his presence being so visible in public. He took charge of the need of his to strengthen the ties with his Haitian side of the family. Reason being, a personal security team was being assembled, one outside of that which would oversee the club. He'd learned from his mistakes of the past and had placed absolute faith and trust in his decisions to do two things: one; not to mix business and pleasure; and two, not to conduct affairs with others outside of family too closely or in depth. The fallout between he and Mr. Raymond opened his eyes to all he was previously blind to.

Mitch had a brother by the name of Noah. He was the one in particular who Mitch designated to be over the majority of all the business affairs in Haiti. Noah's eldest son, Trevino Jean-Pierre Duvalier, aka Haitian Vino, commuted back-and-forth between the States and Haiti on a regular. He'd done so for the past twenty-five years, dating back to a time when he was a teenager. Noah was also the father of Roland. He and Trevino were the closest of Noah's three sons and two daughters.

Trevino was in Haiti on a visit in 2010 during the time that the earthquake hit and destroyed the country. He lost a girlfriend and their twin babies in the devastation. He made the decision to remain there and not return to Miami, Florida so soon, as the obligation to stay and help rebuild and reconstruct the country was taken on by him. The family owned residential and commercial properties all about the capital city, and Trevino, had a stake in everything. They couldn't afford to lose anything behind the civil and political unrest that was to follow, coupled with the tragedy of the quake and the aftermath of it. Prior to, while in the States, Trevino, a star team player behind the uncle, Mitch, had amassed a tremendous level of street power and infamy, through the calculated machinations of his. He had a penchant for murder and mayhem.

Haitian Vino was well known throughout the underworld of Miami. Throughout his rise to power, he was able to thoroughly restructure what was left of the notorious and heavily feared "Zoe Pound" gang. The Feds were able to dismantle the group and put many away in prison. Vino brought back together only the most loyal and the most dedicated members of the enterprise, then paired them with the old elite gangsters of the underworld, the crew that his Uncle Mitch was tied to. Their drug dealings and other money-making rackets operated smoothly.

Vino proved to be a bona fide street general. He headed a segment of the Zoe Pound crew that was thoroughly into the business of robbing cargo freighters that were parked at the docks of the Port of Miami. These were the tugboats that were loaded with large caches of narcotics, most notably cocaine. There was also other contraband taken throughout their heists that the smugglers were attempting to have entered into the black market of the country. This was of course until Haitian Vino and the boys, pulled off a successful strike. Also, this unit of Haitian-Creole goons, carried out hits on rivals and other violators all in the name of the gang they stood for: **Zoe Pound**.

On one such hijacking mission that Vino led, they hit the jackpot. This was the biggest of them all, occurring in the year 2005. The take was two hundred kilos of cocaine. This was enough material to provide them riches to live on for a long time to come following the caper. Vino knew it was best to tone it down a bit with the robberies and be content with the success that came about from the last operation. This was a reckless way of living, and the man of importance that he now was, shouldn't be indulging in anything of such nature, so emphasized the powerful spiritual advisor and elite voodoo priestess, his grandmother. She'd indoctrinated Vino with the thought and belief in himself to foresee his destiny as an honest boss, an influential figure, and a legitimate dynamic force in the world, as opposed to being a peon, a pawn, or a fool that so happened to find a stroke of good luck every once in a while. The grandmother provoked him to be more thoughtful as a leader and a statesman. His individual personality and mind mandated this as well, so she declared. He needed to be more careful instead of carefree. Vino took heed and implemented all that was advised of him to do.

Vino began to invest and move money wisely versus throwing his finances to the wind and potentially placing himself back into the necessity to have to rob again or take on a contract to hit someone to gain money so as to feed his family and support his livelihood.

A connection to a Dominican supplier was explored from that point, and Vino began being provided endless kilos of grade-A quality cocaine to distribute.

Chapter 28

On the back end of the equation, Vino's Uncle Mitch, was tied in with Mr. Raymond, as the two began to dabble with the new wave of narcotics supplied to them by the Mexican cartel leader, El Chucho, due to the decline in the American appetite for cocaine. Mitch and the group of those he was the leader of, sold a little of everything. The streamline to the cocaine source was by and through the nephew, Vino, while the meth and opioids channels, remained intact by and through Mr. Raymond. In addition, Mr. Raymond cultivated an acquaintance with suppliers who worked for the legendary Sinaloa cartel, to be provided large amounts of heroin and Tramadol.

It was the crew that Mitch held authority over that basically got rid of the majority of the drugs they were supplied. In lock step with Mr. Raymond, Mitch utilized the club as well, to clean up the money from the illicit activities. He too owned several small businesses and managed them well to avoid any attention from the government at all costs.

Unfortunately for Vino, the supply line of the cocaine he was provided began to dry up. The national drug task force of the Dominican Republic's government launched an offensive strike campaign in the country targeting all top-level drug lords and were successful. The supplier to Vino was assassinated.

Vino had no back up that he could go to keep the operation flowing. Therefore, he minimized spending and ensured he had millions put away in banks and various safe houses. Also, when he decided to remain in Haiti, this helped too as the price of goods, services, and the cost of living was far less than that of America.

The legitimate businesses owned by Vino and his family turned solid profits, and he lived well from this. Mitch wanted the beloved nephew to return to the States; that way, they could continue to start-up more businesses and keep their family united and strong with Vino as a Capo over the generation of lineage he was around the same age as. The nephew had no problem with this and agreed to return. He made his headquarters there in little Haiti Miami, Florida, while Mitch's office was at the club, K.O.D.

Mitch's grudge with Mr. Raymond continued to carry on even long after the fact. He was so pissed that he'd failed to retrieve the twelve percent principal that was there for him in an escrow account at the bank. Mitch also failed to contact Mr. Raymond anymore and didn't contact the bank either. Therefore, Mr. Raymond figured what the hell! If Mitch didn't want the money, he'd simply take it back. That was exactly what happened. And not only this. To the surprise of Mr. Raymond, to Mitch, and to all the former employees of the club, it was never reopened under a new name or new management by the buyer, Mr. Joel Wynn.

For whatever reasons or due to whatever happened in the process, the building that was once known as King of Dimez, was transformed to a high-end furniture dealer. The parking lot of the place was often rented out to auto show and vehicle auction personnel. Mitch had definitely developed a grand level of malice in his heart toward Mr. Raymond and began contemplating various ways to either kill Mr. Raymond, or, to have him killed for each and every foul thing he'd done. That of the old and that of the new. He plotted night and day, patiently awaiting the chance to strike. This was how Mitch thought of Mr. Raymond, in this regard, as Mr. Raymond of him now.

Mitch became diligent within his contemplation of hindsight. He now took notice from a mental standpoint of everything from a conniving and cutthroat nature that Mr. Raymond had perpetrated against him. It all had culminated into the one big day of which the meeting was held and the club sold. He slowly came to recognize the evil acts that were cast at him for whatever reasons that they were. These thoughts vehemently irked Mitch, prompting him to move faster to get back at Mr. Raymond or to either hit someone close to him. There was a need for the man to relieve himself of the rage that brewed within him. Only God knew what Mitch was subject to do if he was to come to the knowledge of Mr. Raymond now having as a mistress, his wife that he was separated from, Camille.

But Mitch's focus was elsewhere. He had his nephew, Vino, back in the States, alongside him again with their other male family members. They were eager as ever to do work. Mitch summoned everyone on the team to his home for a power conference on how they were to do business and move forward in handling affairs.

Chapter 29

Following a visit at the hospital by police investigators, Calvin thought long and hard over all the photos and surveillance footage he was shown by the detectives. He'd began the process of narrowing things down the best way he could on who it could've possibly been to shoot him. He knew of no one but one particular person, being that there was no one else who loved the Boise State University football team as much as this guy he had in mind.

Calvin even went so far as to get in contact with the female who took his order for food that night to ask her a few things of importance, the girl, Shonda. He questioned her about all the people that visited the restaurant within the hour time frame before he had. There were three people seated and eating at the time he'd entered. Calvin went so far as to describe to Shonda everything about Melvin from—what he remembered—the particular facial features, the way he walked, his size, and his height. Also, Melvin maintained a pair of immaculate hands. He kept really clean nails and ensured that they were thoroughly manicured.

Shonda did confirm something about a particular male customer Calvin inquired about. Melvin loved to wear a thick diamond clustered pinky ring on his left hand. It was an item taken from a guy he and Vick killed in a home invasion gone wrong. This was prior to him going off to prison. Melvin had his mother keep the ring during the time away and retrieved it when he got free. Shonda made Calvin aware that yes, she recalled a guy having a large ring on his pinky, but he was a buffed dude, not someone who Calvin described. Following this, he proceeded to ask others from around the neighborhood who knew of him and Melvin well, if or not they had seen the guy recently. There were a few who said, yes, they had; and there were those that said, no, they hadn't seen the dude, Melvin, in years. Therefore, to be one hundred percent sure of things—was Melvin free or still locked up—Calvin had his sister, Ester, to accompany him and made it his business to take a trip to Melvin's mother's home to know for certain. He was so paranoid in the moment to the point that he had his cell phone at the ready to speed dial 9-1-1 if he was to lay eyes on Melvin there.

Calvin and Ester exited her car and approached the front door. Ester knocked. It was a Thursday around two P.M.

"Who's there?" asked Melvin's mother, Mrs. Irene.

"Um, my name is Ester, ma'am. May I please speak with you for a moment?" responded Ester. The door was opened. She spoke through the burglar bars.

The old lady was in the kitchen preparing a meal at the time the visitors appeared. Once at the front door, Mrs. Irene posed a curious look about her face regarding the two. "Yes. May I help you?" she asked.

"Yes. How are you, ma'am? I'm Ester, and this here is my brother, Calvin." She pointed to him.

Mrs. Irene construed her face as if to strain in memory if she recognized the guy who stood at her door or not. She'd seen him so many times before, but those were times long past. Not to mention that her age prevented her memory from working at its best.

"Would you happen to be Melvin's mother?" Ester asked.

"I might be. Why you ask?" replied Mrs. Irene.

"It's because . . . he's a good friend of ours, and we heard he's finally home from prison. How true is this?"

"For the most part, yes. He has made it home from that place. But my son moved away two days after he got free. That was almost a year ago."

"Oh! He *was* released, I see," Calvin said. This was his first time speaking.

"As I stated, young man, about a year ago. And if I may ask, how long have you two been knowing my son?"

Chapter 30

Calvin wasn't sure if it was a good idea or not to make Mrs. Irene aware of exactly how well he knew Melvin, as he didn't want to trigger her memory to know who he was. She would definitely let Melvin know that it was Calvin who came by looking for him, and this would further complicate the situation of Calvin learning who it was that tried to kill him. So, to avoid this, he related the first thing to come to mind regarding he and Melvin.

"Ma'am, I've known Melvin since the sixth grade," he replied.

"And you say your name is what again, young man?"

"It's Calvin, ma'am."

"That name doesn't ring a bell with me. But anyway, he's not here, and he doesn't live in Miami any longer," Mrs. Irene stated.

"Is there any way you could provide us with a number to reach him, ma'am?" asked Calvin.

"I don't think that'll be possible. Not until I speak to him first about this. However, if you wanna leave a number for him to contact you, it's fine."

"Yes, I can do that, ma'am," Calvin responded to the lady. "Ester, leave her your number please."

The sibling wrote down her number on a small piece of paper. Her name was included. Calvin had another question or so he wanted to ask before they were to leave. "Ma'am, when was the last time that your son visited home, might I ask?"

"Once again, young man, I haven't seen my son since the day he packed up and moved away. He only calls to check in on me. That's about it."

Calvin had a thought. *Either this old bitch is lying to us or she's beginning to develop dementia or something. I know better now. Melvin had to have been the motherfucka who shot me. He's home. And that's no coincidence about the person who I saw in the pictures and video that was wearing the Boise State University hat. It had to be Melvin. He's the only person I can think of. Who else could it have been?*

"Ma'am, next time Melvin calls, could you tell him that Calvin and Ester came by and that we need to speak with him soon?" Calvin asked.

"I certainly shall. The very moment I give him the number you left with me," Mrs. Irene replied.

"We thank you for your time, ma'am, and you take care, okay?" stated Ester.

"You two do the same," the old lady replied then closed the door. The visitors walked back to the car.

Prior to that day, Melvin had long made his mother aware that anytime someone suddenly appeared at the house looking for him for whatever reason, no matter who it was, that she should always tell them that he no longer lived there and had moved away. She followed his instructions. Calvin and Ester were convinced to believe the story. The old lady held true to what was asked of her—that if anyone didn't call first to notify her they would be coming by, most likely, they had not been invited to pay them a visit. "Don't let no one inside, especially if you're home alone. And don't entertain too much conversation from them," he said to his mother. Mrs. Irene kept this in mind at the approach of the recent visitors.

PART TWO

Chapter 31

The intended target was contacted and befriended on social media by someone that posed as a female who was attracted to him. The person doing this contacting, desired to communicate and begin to get to know one another until they were potentially comfortable enough to go out on a date. The person doing the reaching out maintained information and other details on Facebook that could very well be false and placed there as a set up to something else. And due to the fact that Big Mix was so gullible and weak for women, he'd be more than willing to get to know any female through message exchanges.

He only wanted to be accepted. The man long struggled with inferiority issues and low self-esteem the majority of his life, and was prone to being rejected by females, no matter what he had to offer. This was most likely the reason why he'd chosen to be a bouncer at strip clubs. He found this to be a better way to get close to females and work his mojo to get sex out of them—pay to play arrangements basically.

Without having a thorough knowledge of who it was he was communicating with, Big Mix foolishly provided the supposed female with the address to his place of residence for them to appear at a later date for the two to go out for a night on the town. Prior to this, Big Mix was under the impression that maybe he was being bullshitted by the female in a way, due to them never having a verbal conversation, only messages exchanged. But then, the correspondent offered to buy Big Mix gifts so as to eliminate any form of suspicion that he may have. A nice outfit of a shirt, tie, slacks, and dress shoes, were ordered and sent to the address he'd already provided. This made the plot far easier to carry out.

The hired hitter planted himself outside of Big Mix's house and sought out ways to creep into the domain to take him out and complete the contract. He was well trained and groomed by one of the best killers that Miami had ever cultivated. Lock picking was an art that he specialized in. This came with the profession.

The time was 10:10 P.M. Night was fully set in. Big Mix's new location was in Wellington, Florida, a quiet town that wasn't heavily populated, not too far from Fort Lauderdale. Since the kidnapping, the beating, and the robbery, along with the situation he'd incurred after the fact with Mr. Raymond, he decided to exit Miami for a time being to get his mind together and allow Mr. Raymond the opportunity to overcome the anger and resentment he had toward him. Once this was to take place, the two may be able to talk and gain an understanding again.

Big Mix had given up the large SUVs he once favored for an ordinary, smaller, more gas efficient car to take him back-and-forth. The car wasn't parked at the house. The hitter knew of a sure way to know the whereabouts of the big fella. As he sat in a nearby brush of bushes, he pulled out the prepaid cell phone that was used to pose as the female who communicated with Big Mix on social media. To Big Mix, it was "Melissa" he was in contact with.

MELISSA: *Jerome. How are you today?*

A couple of minutes later, Big Mix replied.

BIG MIX: *I'm blessed. And you?*

MELISSA: *I'm good. Just sitting here thinking about you. About us, actually.*

BIG MIX: *Oh, really! That's nice to know. But look. I'm gonna have to text you later when I get home. Okay, sweetie?*

I'm at the gym now. And I gotta stop by the grocery store on my way home. Give me about an hour, okay?

MELISSA: *Okay. Take care.*

From that point, the perpetrator immediately went to work in breaking into the home of Big Mix. It took no more than six minutes to gain entry. A walk-through was performed. He opened closets and made a full assessment of the entirety of the house. Note was taken of the CPAP breathing machine and a bottle of extra strength sleeping pills that rested on the nightstand next to the bed.

I'm sure that this nigga is gonna be good and knocked out when I make my return to kill his ass, thought the hired goon. A small corner portion of the curtain in the bedroom was created by the hitter to make a peephole view of the bedroom from the outside when the time was to arrive for him to return. Before the intruder exited the house, he was sure to unlatch the window in the kitchen that rested over the sink. The backdoor was rigged as well to make access easy once more. The premises was departed at that point. The hitter was ready and set to return five hours later to officially put Big Mix away forever.

Chapter 32

The time reached 3:22 A.M. The hitter was armed with a Glock .40 pistol, a seven-inch ice pick, and a Bowie knife to get the job over and done with in a successful fashion. He made his entry into the house yet again through the backdoor. Before doing so, he'd taken a look through the bedroom window and observed Big Mix sound asleep atop the bed, lying on his left side with his back to the door of the room. The mask to the CPAP machine was strapped to his head and covered his face. The inside of the house was slightly dark. The light from the TV was the only illumination throughout the room.

The clothing of the intruder was black. He had on a ski mask to disguise his face. The killer tiptoed down the narrow hallway and eased open the door to Big Mix's bedroom. His back was still to the door. The assassin felt the urge to work fast and efficiently. He knew not to lag around long or to make too much noise. His kills had to be clean and quick. The sharp pointed ice pick was withdrawn. A ferocious grimace was formed on the face of the intruder behind the mask. He walked over to Big Mix. With no show of hesitation or mercy, he rammed the weapon's tip deep into the skull of Big Mix, just behind the right ear. The brain was punctured. Death was instant.

The malicious, coldblooded killer then whipped out the knife he had and slit the throat of Big Mix from ear to ear. The blade was buried deep into the flesh. He then flicked the excess blood onto the wall, wiped the weapons with the blanket of the bed, put them back along the waistline, and strutted out the house the same way he'd entered. Silent as ever was the "Silent Assassin". This was Willie, the bodyguard for Mr. Raymond.

Chapter 33

Melvin's cousin, Vick, had reached out to him and made him aware that everything was in place for them to do a run to the north in the next week to come. They needed to go over the details of the mission.

"Hello!" Melvin answered his phone.

"What's good, fam? How you?" Vick asked.

"Everything is all good on my end. What about you?"

"Busy, busy, busy, I tell you. But look. We need to meet up. You already know I'm not gonna do all this talking over the phone," Vick stated.

"Okay. Cool. When?" Melvin wanted to know.

"Now if you're available."

"I am."

"I'm at my girl, LuLu's, house. I'mma text you the address, okay?"

"Bet that. I'll be on my way once I get it. I got some shit to tell you too, fam. You not gonna believe this," Melvin declared.

"Word!" Vick responded.

"Word, my nigga. I'll fill you in when I get there. I'm at Traci's spot now. She went to work not long ago. I'm getting around now in a little low budget rental. Had to park the truck for a minute."

"Just come on to see me, and we can talk about everything," said Vick

"Bet," Melvin quickly responded. The call concluded. He got dressed then and there in the present moment and made his way to see Vick.

One hour later, Melvin was there at LuLu's house having a conversation with his cousin.

"So, yeah, cuz." Melvin began to relate something of importance to Vick. "How about, my mom tells me that some guy and his sister came by the house and so-called themselves looking for me, asking questions and the whole nine, my nigga!"

"Oh, yeah?! Who the fuck was it?!" Vick asked.

"Nigga, you not gonna believe this."

"Who, fam?"

"It was that nigga, Calvin Prescott, and his sister, Ester!" Melvin revealed.

"Get the fuck outta here, nigga! What the fuck he doing coming by your mom's place? Trying to apologize or something?! And what the fuck was the nigga's sister doing with him? Was you smashing the bitch or something before you got locked up?"

"Nah, cuz. I don't know what the fuck that nigga wanted. Beats the hell outta me."

"Didn't that nigga get shot or something like that not too long ago? I thought I'd heard this correctly from a reliable source."

"Yeah. He did. And that's what the problem is, cuz. I didn't manage to kill the nigga! He was lucky that night," Melvin revealed.

"Oh! So now I know where we going with this. What the fuck happened? How you wasn't able to bump him off?" Vick inquired.

"I know I hit him and got him good. But, somehow, he didn't die. I wasn't able to kill him," Melvin related.

"Yeah, I heard that too . . . that somebody got him good. But as you say, he ain't die. You don't think that by he and his sister stopping by the house, got anything to do with him being shot, do you?"

"I doubt it because, with me knowing him the way I do, he would've brought the police with him too, if that was the case," Melvin gave his thoughts.

"Yeah, you might be right about that one there. But Melvin, I still gotta know. How the fuck you wasn't able to kill that fool, fam? It's no way he's supposed to still be breathing."

"Shit, I got off eleven shots. But only four hit him. All I can say is that he was lucky that night. That's it. He got lucky to walk away with his life."

"You didn't lose any shells, did you?"

"Nah. I used the plastic bag method. And when I got home, I flushed them all down the toilet. So, I'm good on that end."

"Well, that's all that matters. And Calvin probably didn't want anything. Must've heard you were out and wanted to see for himself to be sure. Nothing to worry about. Like you said, if it was, the police would've been the one to pay you a visit. Not him and his sister. But anyway, moving on to other things. Check it out. We got a hundred and thirty-seven pieces that need to be picked up. There's twenty AKs, fifty 9-millimeters of all types, Glocks, Berettas, .45s, AR-15s, revolvers, and others. We got three stops to make once we get up north—one in Philly, one across the bridge in Camden; and I got to see my nigga, Fat Tony, up in Harlem. You know me and him always have a good time when we get together. The both of us love them dogs, cuz," Vick related to Melvin in an excited way.

"Oh, he's the one you got those game bred fighting ass dogs from, right?" asked Melvin.

"Yep! He's my dog man. I'm connected too," Vick replied, rubbing his hands together energetically for emphasis.

"I remember the pictures and videos all too well that you sent to my phone I had when I was locked up. You and dude were in matches."

Chapter 34

The conversation continued between the two. Vick said, "I just remembered something too. You may have the opportunity to see a couple of those matches live now, since you're free. Tony got a show coming up. It's gonna take place during the time we're up the way. Them niggaz be betting some serious money too, cuz. We're gonna be able to splurge throughout the time we're there, from the money off the guns."

"Shit, I'm with that all day, cuz," said Melvin.

"But yeah, Melvin, when we get on our way, we make a stop in Valdosta, Georgia for a pickup. It's directly along our route. I've got a couple of niggaz out of V-Town, Moultrie, Georgia, and Albany, Georgia that's gonna meet up with us at the mall there to deliver what they got. Then, we head on up I-75 to ATL, connect with my niggaz there, and get the rest of the goods. From that point, we hit the highway again, cut across the Carolinas, hop on I-95, and continue on our journey up. You feeling me on that?"

"So, how long we gonna be away?"

"About a week. Maybe two. I've got a down ass girlfriend I met on one of my runs, who lives in New York. We ain't got to worry about hotel fees and other expenses. Me and shorty got a place together," Vick stated.

"Oh, you got you a female out the Big Apple, huh?" Melvin inquired with a smile.

"No doubt about that, family. She's deep too, cuz, in terms of being knowledgeable about self. She helps me see life in a different way and live better. I'm thankful for her. And of course, you know those up north females love themselves those thorough dudes from down south like us. We've got a tight bond and video chat on the phone almost daily."

"If she's got this type of effect upon you, I can't wait to meet her. I'm sure she has to be a special kind of lady to help you elevate and change for the better. Not saying that you're not already a good dude, but, I've never heard you speak like this before about a female," Melvin said to Vick.

Vick took a look at him and returned the smile behind the compliment. "Indeed, there are certain females that have a certain type of appeal about themselves to cause a man with a stone heart to become more kind and humble."

"To be honest with you, fam, I always thought you would go on to marry LuLu at some point."

"Me and LuLu still good too. It's just that the other one . . ."

"The other one what, fam? I need to hear this, because you and LuLu been holding strong now almost twenty years. Y'all got a daughter together and all. And by the way, what's the name of the New York girl? You never said," Melvin cut him off mid-sentence to say.

"Her name is Sakinah, cuz," Vick revealed.

"Sakinah! That name sounds exotic in a way. What's the meaning of it?"

"She said that her name represents calmness, tranquility, and reassurance. But you'll come to know more about her once we get there. Just be prepared to leave in the next few days."

Chapter 35

"I will. But check this out, cuz. About this whole Calvin situation. What's the best thing I need to do about it? What would you suggest? Because now, I feel like the nigga may be subject to show up again at my mom's doorsteps, and that's not good for business as I move forward," Melvin asked.

"I really thought you'd never ask. But truth be, when we go away on our journey to the north, I'll be sure to take care of that for you, fam. I know a hitter or two I can call on to get the job done. And you're my cousin, Melvin. You're now a part of my business that I have going. I don't need no interference by no one, especially not by a lame ass, nobody ass nigga like he is! A nigga who should've been dead years ago. So, without too much more elaboration on the subject, dude has got to go! Plain and simple. He's a nuisance and must be eradicated!" Vick stated in an emphatic manner.

"Well, say no more on that, fam. It's understood. Just hit me up when it's time for us to move out, a'ight?" Melvin stated then stood to his feet in preparation to leave.

"I will," Vick replied, getting to his feet as well. "Be sure to tell Auntie I said hello."

"Absolutely," Melvin concluded. They dapped hands and embraced. Melvin then made his way out the door to head back to Traci's house.

Melvin was anxious as ever to hit the road and get back to work moving firearms. Vick was able to instil a level of confidence in him that was necessary to ensure that everything was intact and holding strong. The team had to be solid, and all fear needed to be eliminated for the only thing there was to fear, was fear itself. Nothing more.

Chapter 36

An important meeting between Mr. Raymond and a friend/business partner took place. There was a need to discuss the order of affairs related to the enterprise of theirs. A strange occurrence had taken effect regarding this particular powwow. It was something that had never been so prior. Mr. Raymond brought along a third party to attend. For whatever was the reason that Mr. Raymond saw fit, he brought Felicia with him to play the role of secretary instead of having the successor nephew tag along to link with Emanuel and have the opportunity to relate to one another how they were to interact moving forward.

Felicia was allowed to sit in and be provided the exclusive details on some of everything the slowly retiring narcotics czar and close associate talked about. This may have been a potentially damning mistake on Mr. Raymond's behalf as too much trust and too much confidentiality was placed in Felicia entirely too fast. Regardless of what, Mr. Raymond felt no harm was done nor would any come his way. He initiated the conversation. They were at the main funeral parlor owned by Emanuel.

"Emanuel, what's up?! How you been, my brother?" Mr. Raymond greeted upon entering the back room space of the mortuary where Emanuel sat. He and Felicia were holding hands. It was late in the evening. Emanuel was there alone. Everyone else had already gone for the day. However, there were two corpses stretched out on tables that were being prepped for eternal rest and were totally nude. Felicia became horrified in a way, palming Mr. Raymond by the wrist very tightly with both her hands. Instead of it being a Friday night in the city lights, it became a "fright night" upon first sight for her.

Emanuel looked from Mr. Raymond to Felicia then back again. A look of astonishment overtook his face. He absolutely couldn't believe what he was led to believe in all that he observed. The elder buddy squinted his eyes and pouted his lips. "Ray, what in the world are you thinking? Or are you even thinking? Because I don't know about this." He protested the presence of Felicia.

"Relax, Emanuel. Everything is fine. This here is my new secretary," Mr. Raymond responded and put his arm around the girl's neck. "She's gonna be one of the main people to help put together a great campaign team that shall see to it that yours truly becomes mayor. I need her by my side and involved to help me keep track and stay on top of things. This was the same way it was done at the club," he stated, leaning over and gently stroking Felicia along the cheekbone.

"If you say so, man. If you say so." Emanuel worded it twice so as to thoroughly give caution. "All I know is that your brother, Phillip, he never allowed no one to be present in any conversation that he and I would have about our business."

"I'm not my brother, Emanuel. And, as I've said, we're good. I promise you on this," Mr. Raymond retorted. He then gestured with a hand to urge Emanuel to get on with what they'd met up to talk over.

"Well, you're the boss, so here we go," Emanuel let out then proceeded. "All the money is accounted for with *Baskin-Robbins*." This was a nickname for the street drug, meth. It was also called "ice cream," due to the many colorful forms of products made with it when included. "We had a return profit of . . ." Emanuel took a pause mid-sentence. A bit of scorn was now attached to his facial features. He continued. "Baskin-Robbins returned a total of . . ." He paused yet again before spitting out any numbers.

Chapter 37

Emanuel took a hard look at Raymond. He had daggers in his eyes in doing so. Pity also filled his heart behind the thought of what could go wrong in talking in the presence of a complete stranger. This was Felicia to him. "As I was saying, Baskin-Robbins returned a total of $8,000,000. My favorite aunt, Geneva's, medicine cabinet and all the opioids that were left, returned $3,000,000. I counted $10,000,000 from the sale of all we had left over to be sold, plus the $5,000,000 we keep put away for emergency purposes. Of course, this is located in the hole where my buddy, Amos, takes a piss." He was referring to an underground safe that was beneath the doghouse to his pet Doberman Pinscher. "This gives a total of $26,000,000 after sweeping the floor and airing out the laundry," Emanuel related in a somber tone. He looked on at Felicia with a menacing stare.

"That's amazing, Emanuel. You're the best, my guy. Now, we've got to take about $3,000,000 of that and put it toward the campaign team until I begin to raise money as a candidate. We've got to pay staff and purchase material to gain the attention of the voters. Also, next week, I'm gonna have Felicia here stop back through to pick up a half million from you, so she could go ahead and create the website and other social media platforms so healthy dialogue can take place. We've got to get people registered. Felicia will have the duty to hire her own assistants, and then, they all will do their part to establish trust in us with the people and secure votes," Mr. Raymond stated to Emanuel.

"So, this young lady right here," he pointed to Felicia, "is technically your campaign manager, right?" Emanuel asked.

"That's correct, Emanuel. Felicia is to me what the loyal and dedicated Kellyanne Conway was to our dear president, Donald J. Trump. From the beginning of the campaign as the manager, to what she is now in 2019," Mr. Raymond properly explained to his friend. "I trust in her to do a really good job, my brother. And I've got to rent a building or something soon to host a dinner party. It's got to be to gather a delegation and begin raising funds that will ensure a successful campaign run. I intend to make my official announcement at that time. My honorable mentions as well, which would include you, Emanuel," Mr. Raymond said with a smile.

The remark related to him being mentioned honorably seemed to lighten the old man's mood. A smile appeared upon his face.

Mr. Raymond spoke further. "Oh, yeah, Felicia, we've got to also be sure to book plenty of airtime on the radio and have ad space from TV networks. An appeal has to be made to the diverse group of voters that our city is known to cater to. We're open to acceptance to all people who believe in my message and the policies I shall implement beginning my very first day in office."

"I've made note of this already, sweetie, and have contacted the necessary companies to put them on notice of what we're looking to do soon," Felicia spoke up.

'You see how amazing she is, Emanuel?" Mr. Raymond said with a bright smile about his face. "She's indispensable. I'll never get rid of her. Felicia has been an asset to me since day one, the day she was recruited and brought to the club to work. She immediately caught my attention. We've got to have a pretty face and a smart woman to speak to the press. And Felicia—my beautiful secretary—is always on point. I thank you so much, sweetie," Mr. Raymond stated then leaned over to kiss Felicia.

Emanuel gave Mr. Raymond a perplexed look behind his actions. It was as if to say, *Well, damn! Whatever happened to the wife and daughter that you have at home?* He spoke at that point. "It sounds good to me, my brother. It sounds good. But on another note, what happened with the you know what, that you know who, had picked up, but never made it to where it was supposed to make it to?" he questioned about Big Mix, the pills, and the money in code.

"Oh, that . . . It's taken care of. I called on someone to properly rectify the situation. It was just that simple to resolve. But anyway, I have strong reason to believe that we're gonna make it, my brother. I can promise you on that. We're gonna make it," Mr. Raymond proclaimed.

"Oh, yeah! We definitely are," Felicia chimed in to say.

The meeting ended. Mr. Raymond and Felicia went on about their business, leaving Emanuel to do the same. Mr. Raymond had no knowledge of the fact that each time he left his home, he was being followed and photographed. His wife, Christine, hired a private investigator to keep tabs on him to establish an evidential basis as to why their divorce was necessary and why the enormous amount of money in alimony she would request should be granted.

In addition to the marital issues, other problems began to mount and was subject to plague Mr. Raymond. A devastating blow was dealt to his organization in regard to the underworld activities he headed. These set of problems began at the time he instructed Yolanda to go by the funeral parlor to meet Emanuel and pick up the money owed to her.

Yolanda's contact with Emanuel, triggered a broader investigation that now included the old man. His ties to Mr. Raymond created this. A wiretap warrant was requested and eventually secured by the government. They had sufficient probable cause. Emanuel's landlines and wireless communication devices were bugged. Roughly two weeks after the day Yolanda appeared to retrieve the cash, a team of highly trained and effective technicians from the FBI, broke into the funeral parlor and secretly planted four electronic eavesdropping microphones throughout the establishment. Emanuel was now compromised. To add further insult to injury, the private room where he, Mr. Raymond, and Felicia held their conversation, contained a listening bug. Everything that was said was recorded. This pulled back the curtain more to expose the illegal operation that Mr. Raymond led. Evidence was piling on. One grave mistake was made after another.

Chapter 38

Melvin received a phone call from a number that he didn't readily recognize. He ignored it. A text message followed from the same number. There displayed a code of some sort in it. It read:

K.O.D.'s MAIN MAN # 1.

Melvin knew then and there who it was that was attempting to contact him. No doubt, it was Mr. Raymond. This was his way to identify himself to the former security personnel at the club. Indeed, it was the real boss looking to connect. As for the specific icon he used—the hashtags—these were assigned to inform Melvin that the boss intended to speak directly to him. All the other bouncers at the time had different icons attached to their method of communications. Melvin called at this point.

"Ray here," Melvin's former boss answered.

"Hey, Mr. Raymond! Long time having the chance to speak to you," Melvin responded.

"Yeah, I know. I've been really busy of late. But nonetheless, if I'm calling to talk with you, it must be of importance."

"I'm sure that it has to be. And this is probably one of the main reasons why I never changed my phone number once you sold the club and moved on to other things. I've had the same one since I got free, and you, being the first one to accept me and place me on your team. And I'm a man of my word. I pledge my loyalty and allegiance to you, Mr. Ray. I can't thank you nearly enough for what you done for me," Melvin stated.

"And I'm a man of mine, Melvin. Like I told you before, I admire you and respect your style, and the ambition and drive that you have. But above all, I appreciate the level of reverence that you've always held for me. So, on the strength of this alone—based on what you've shown me—I want to keep you onboard for the new voyage I'm destined to sail upon. And hopefully, I'll be able to transcend to greater levels throughout my endeavors. Because what I want is, I'd like to have you tag along with me as well, Melvin," Mr. Raymond responded with a bit of praise for the young protégé.

"It would be both an honor and a pleasure, Mr. Ray, so long as it's not another club security gig again."

"Nah! It's no more of that for me, Melvin. I'm done with the clubbing industry, my guy. It's time for ol' Ray-Ray Stephens here, to play a different game for bigger stakes now. No more small fish in a frying pan for me. I've moved up to a top notch rung on the ladder of success," Mr. Raymond boasted.

"Oh, yeah! That's right. I do recall hearing something about you taking aim at being the mayor of the city," commented Melvin.

"That's correct. I'm aiming high to be the mayor."

"But Mister Ray, I've been meaning to ask you something."

"What's that, Melvin?"

"What's the deal between you and Mitch? What y'all got going on, may I ask?"

"It was a plain and simple remedy to the issues that the both of us experienced. I was no longer having any growth or prosperity with him as a business partner. And I got tired of the club thing. I envisioned myself to be better and greater than I was. Therefore, I pulled the plug on it all and sold out to the highest bidder," Mr. Raymond related.

"I was wondering about that, because, there was so much talk going on around our group about this and about that, to the point where I didn't know what to believe throughout the entire fiasco," Melvin stated.

"A *fiasco*, you say, huh? Ha-ha-ha-ha! That's a nice choice of a word there, Melvin. I like how you put it. But anyway, Mitch had began to swagger around like he was the sole owner of the place, and also, tried to dictate too much. So, I let homeboy have it," Mr. Ray declared.

Chapter 39

"Okay. Understood. But on another note, did you happen to hear the news about Big Mix?" Melvin asked.

"Yeah, I heard. It's a damn shame how someone killed the man. The way it was described in how they found his body, it had to have been some random female he may had welcomed into his house. Jerome was a wild boy when it came to the girls," Mr. Raymond replied. "They say the police has no leads nor any potential suspects as to who it was that done it. His sister sent me an email to let me know about the situation. I donated money for his funeral. I wasn't able to make it, but I did provide flowers and food. May his soul rest in peace," Mr. Raymond further said.

"Yeah. May his soul rest in peace," Melvin repeated.

"But I'm curious to know, why you asked about Mitch."

"Oh, that! It wasn't nothing too serious. He and I had a conversation since. He also had me to meet up with him a few weeks ago."

"Oh, yeah? What is it ol' Mitch talking about these days?"

"He said something about he was in the process of buying a building of his own to turn into a club, and that he was in the process of putting together a team of security men for it. This was why he ended up getting in touch with me, to know if or not I might be interested in a part-time post three days out the week," Melvin revealed.

"And your answer to that was?" Mr. Raymond wanted to know.

"I went on ahead and told him yeah, that I was interested. So long as the pay was gonna be right, and since it wouldn't be no more than three days out of the week, no more than six hours each night."

"*Ah, ha-ha-ha-ha!* That Mitch. He's a really funny dude, you know." Mr. Raymond found it comical of the fact in what his former business partner was trying to do. "That dude is always busy trying to outdo me. That's just not gonna happen. It's just not. And where is this new building he was contemplating on buying?" Mr. Raymond asked.

"He mentioned something about the old Club Ice building. The blue one on Seventy-ninth Street and Seventh Avenue," Melvin revealed.

"What?!" Mr. Raymond let out with a bit of dismay and humor about his face. "Are you serious, Melvin? Mitch, please give me a break from laughing at you already. But come to think about it, he probably don't have enough money no way to do any better." Mr. Raymond couldn't make himself stop having Mitch at the butt of every joke of his. "But for real, Melvin, man, please don't waste your time giving it a thought to join up with that guy. I won't dare allow a good dude like you to go out bad by dealing with a chump like Mitch. What in the hell is wrong with you, Melvin, for even giving that a consideration?"

"Why you say it like that, Mister Ray?"

"It's because . . . a guy like you . . . you're only supposed to donate your time and services to real boss figureheads. Not someone like Mitch! And remember this if nothing else . . . When on the path to becoming a boss, you only should want to be the companion of a boss. Nothing less. You get me on that?!" he stated.

"Yeah, I got you on that. But Mister Ray, let me ask you this. The both of you bought the building together for what came to be the club, right?"

"Correct. But I put more money into it than he had, which made me, the CEO and him, the COO."

"Okay. I understand now."

"So, let me ask you this, Melvin. And maybe you can see it better from the angle I give it to you from. How many times have you ever called Mitch, boss?"

"Shit never! Not from what I recall," Melvin replied.

"Okay. Now, how many times have you acknowledged me as, boss?" Mr. Raymond specifically asked.

"Many times, Mister Ray. And you're the first person to give me a job when I came home, and afforded me the chance to make honest money."

"Now you seem to get my point."

"I do, Mister Ray. But all that aside, what you got lined up for me?" Melvin urged him to reveal the true reason for the call.

"And now you finally ask. You know there had to be more to it for me—the real boss—to reach out."

"Yeah, you're right."

Chapter 40

Mr. Raymond now begin to thoroughly explain his need for Melvin at this point moving forward. "Okay, look. Here's what I got. Jerome, aka Big Mix, is no longer with us. And, I've got to have somebody to replace him moving forward. Of course, I've got another guy who's my right-hand. But there's a need for two. I was moving you closer to me for a reason, Melvin. It was because, I had the proper vision to foresee the future, and knew that you were on your way to make well in it. So, to truly convince you to come roll alongside me, I'm willing to double whatever offer that Mitch has already made you. How does that sound?" Mr. Raymond stated.

"You wanna know something, Mister Ray?"

"What's that?"

"Mitch ain't throwing no offers my way. He never mentioned any numbers," Melvin made him aware.

"Well, how about this? I'm willing to lay forty thousand on you upfront. And you'll be in position to make every bit of ninety grand a year, plus an appreciation bonus from yours truly. Hell, I may even throw in one of my luxury rides for you, being that you'll be my primary driver from here on out." Mr. Raymond was so serious with all he was saying to Melvin.

"I see you're making me an offer that I can't refuse. There's no way I can pass that up. And besides, I don't think Mitch is ready to make an offer to top that. You've been my boss since day one. I have no choice but to keep things the way that they have been."

"That's the way I like to hear my people talk. Human relations is a skill I learned long ago," Mr. Raymond let out to acknowledge all that his new protégé put in perspective.

"Once we're done talking, I'mma text Mitch to let him know I won't be able to join him on the new venture he's looking to start."

"And a strong word of advice . . . be sure to tell him *exactly* why! A real man always speaks a word that's direct toward the truth. Don't hold anything back. Tell him specifically that I made you a better offer to continue working *with* me, not *for* me any longer."

"I plan to do just that, Mister Ray. I ain't no weak dude. I don't bite my tongue when it comes to saying what's needed to be said," Melvin stated with a tone of authority.

"Good. And I need for you to save this number here in your phone. This will be our direct line to communicate. I'll be back in touch soon. I'm gonna need you to take a ride up the interstate to meet me when I do. It's to my home away from home. Only my right-hand knows the location. Jerome did, but that's no more. Yolanda had always spoken highly of you, Melvin, whether you knew this or not. She encouraged that I keep you on with me at all costs. And that's what I'm doing," Mr. Raymond said.

"Whatever happened with her? How has she been? It seems like she fell from the face of the earth." Melvin felt the need to inquire about the female friend he'd long had an attraction to. They hadn't communicated in a long time.

"Last I heard from her, she was doing well. She said something to the effect of moving back to the Big Easy for the time being to help out with her family there. I paid her what was owed, and that was that. But just be on standby for a call from me. I'll be getting with you soon, my guy."

"Okay, Mister Ray. You take care."

"Likewise, young brother, likewise. And be sure to keep in mind when the time comes, to get out and encourage people to vote **Raymond Eugene Stephens** for mayor."

"That's a bet, Mister Ray. I'll be sure to do that. Be easy," Melvin lastly stated. The call came to an end at that point.

Melvin hadn't anticipated for things to fall in place with Mr. Raymond as they had. Nonetheless, they did. He found himself glad that they went in this way being that the situation helped him put things in perspective and opened his eyes to the raw reality of the world he played in. The only reason that Melvin had previously made the temporary decision to get down with Mitch and all he was aiming to do was because, he was having a sexual affair with the man's daughter and saw an opportunity to get ahead by the dealings that they were involved with. He wanted to gain all that he could from her regarding all she had to provide.

Through Tisha, Melvin was afforded a way to have a hand into the world that Mitch dabbled in, without necessarily doing too much. But then, along came Mr. Raymond once more, making a cloudy situation clear for Melvin. Why begin calling Mitch boss now at this point, when he'd never done so at any time in the past? This made sense to him and became the eye opener to help him see things for what they were, not for how some attempted to make them out to be. Mr. Raymond made a valid point by all measures. Melvin understood the wisdom in the words.

Therefore, according to Mr. Raymond to Melvin, *on his path to becoming a boss, he must first be the companion to one.* This said everything to Melvin that he needed to hear. And Mr. Raymond, began to take initial steps to draw Melvin in further unto his orbit. Melvin felt he couldn't go wrong being in Mr. Raymond's circle. But sometimes, a gut feeling could signal the wrong thing.

Chapter 41

One Day Later . . .

Melvin contacted Tisha to let her know what his new intentions were now to do. He would have to renege on the verbal agreement that was previously made with Mitch. Melvin felt he wouldn't be technically reneging in this sense, being that he hadn't appeared on the job not once, and also, hadn't been provided any money by the man. He was sure that based on the type of guy that Mitch was, a problem was subject to arise behind him backing out. But the bottom line to this was that business was better when it was to be done with Mr. Raymond as opposed to Mitch. And Melvin had nothing to do with the conflict that was going on between the two.

Mitch can be pissed about it all he wants. There is no way I could've turned down the money and the opportunity offered to me by Mr. Ray, a man that I see is clearly moving on up in the world as a boss, Melvin thought.

Tisha's phone rang. She knew who it was by the name that appeared as a contact. A smile came across her face. She rushed to answer. "Hello, baby! How you been?" she greeted.

"I've been good, sweetheart. And yourself?" Melvin responded.

"Life's been good. I can't complain. However, I still can't seem to understand why am I not able to talk to you on a regular or have the opportunity to see you as much as I'd like to? Why can't I be just as important to you as the other woman is who you have in your life? But that's a conversation I'm willing to save for another day. I just adore you, Melvin, and want to be close to you at every chance that I get," Tisha was sure to relate to him. The way that her words came off, it was as if she had this to say held in her mind for a long time. She anticipated what Melvin's response would be.

Damn! This bitch sounds just like Traci with all that. "Tisha, look, I can promise you on this. Whenever the time is right, we're gonna be together and do all the things you wanna do and more. I just need for you to be patient and trust in nature to bring us closer together. A'ight? I'm yours, sweetie. I ain't going nowhere. Okay?" His reply was enough to appease her in the way that he felt it would.

"That's all I needed to know. I simply wanna be assured that everything we have going on won't be all for nothing. But what's on your mind? Talk to me."

"Listen, I know you may not like the sound of what I'm about to tell you—"

Tisha cut his words short. "Baby! Please don't give me any bad news," she stated to him.

"Nah, sweetie. It's not bad news, per se. Not in that sense of the words," he let out.

"So, it must be something that you're in disagreement with my dad about, huh? From the meeting that you two had? He told me about it. My dad was happy to have had a positive conversation with you. He said he was looking forward to more of the same as y'all progress," Tisha made him aware.

"I understand all that, Tisha. I really do. But truth be, the agreement that me and your dad had verbally came to— about me being a bouncer at the new club—won't be able to get involved any longer. Something new and better came up," Melvin brought to her attention.

Tisha took a pause to process all that he had said. She then responded. "Melvin, what do you mean by that?" Clarity was demanded.

"What do you mean by asking me, what I mean by that?' he retorted. "I mean all that I just said: I'm not gonna be able to be a bouncer at your dad's new spot once he open it up. Something new and better came about." He managed to repeat his words.

"Melvin . . . you wanna tell me why you backing out on my dad so fast the way you are? Please tell me, because this isn't cool. Not at all. My dad accepted your word that you'd be a part of his team of men, and he's depending on you to keep true to your word. But now this," Tisha stated. She seemed to vent in a way. Her tone of voice was aggressive, like she'd been offended as well by Melvin's revelation.

"Tisha! Why you seem to be getting all hostile on me?!"

"It's because, Melvin . . . I had to work like hell to get us to that point. And my dad tends to like you as a person. Not to mention the fact that you and I got something deep going on. My dad knows. He's okay with it. He approves of it. Why would we run the risk to ruin the good thing that we have? Especially so soon?"

"Tisha, I'm more than sure your dad won't have a hard time finding someone else to fill the void he had on reserve for me. And that has nothing to do with you and I," Melvin said.

Chapter 42

"Oh, yes dafuq it does! It has *everything* to do with it! When it comes to my father being cool with somebody that I'm involved with, that has so much to do with how my relationship with that significant other will go after a fallout with my dad occurs by that special someone. You get my point?" Tisha expressed. A bout of anxiety was clearly setting in.

"Well, he's gonna have to stay his ass out of our business then, if we're planning to continue with dealing with each other. Of course, this is once I say what's needed to be said to him about my decision to do business otherwise," Melvin said to her.

"Melvin, please don't tell me that you're becoming a contradiction to your own words, are you? That's the type of actions that a grimy dude would take on. And that's not you, I wouldn't want to believe."

"What's that supposed to mean? Why you say it like that?" Melvin responded.

"It's because . . . not long ago, you just said you're not going nowhere and that you're mine. I took you as being honest and sincere on that. And now, it's if we are to continue to deal with each other and all this other crap! What part of *us* is this at this point?" Tisha asked furiously.

"What I mean is that, if you plan on allowing your dad to continue to dictate to you who you can and can't be with, all because the person you're now dealing with gets a better offer to do business with someone else . . . one that's better than what he made . . . then that's not good for you and me on no accord, with this relationship that we share. That's what I mean." Melvin was emphatic with the way he stated his words. Tisha got the message: He was serious.

"Look, is it any way you can come by the house later? I wanna see you. And I feel like this is a conversation that we need to have in person," Tisha stated.

"Oh, so now you finally ready for me to stop by your house, huh!? What if your daddy finds out that I'd been there? Better yet, what if he decides to stop by and sees that I'm there? Then what?"

"Melvin, please! Stop being ridiculous. And why you trying to hurt me anyway?" she asked of him, then began to cry. Her sobs were heard through the phone.

"I'm not trying to hurt you, Tisha. Not in no type of way. I'm just stating the facts for you. If you and I are gonna be together, your father is not gonna have anything to do with our business. Do I make myself clear on that?!" He demanded an answer.

"Melvin, please, just come by my house later, will you? That way we can talk about all of this. Okay?" An attempt was made by her to avoid a reply to the demand placed upon her. Melvin wasn't having it.

"Tisha, do I make myself clear on what I said?!" he repeated.

"Yes, Melvin. Yes, you do. Now come by my house later, please. Okay? Are you?

"I will. Text me your address. And I'll see you later."

"Okay, baby. I will. See you later," Tisha lastly responded. The call came to an end.

A thought raced through Melvin's mind. *Do I call Mitch now and tell him what I need to first, or do I wait until I leave Tisha's house before I do?* His better sense of judgment suggested that he wait until he'd left Tisha's house, being that there stood a good possibility that Mitch would certainly call his daughter after the fact and order her not to ever fuck with him again, due to Melvin reneging on the agreement that they had in place.

Melvin didn't think that him backing out of a verbal agreement was a serious thing—which truth be told probably wasn't—but the fact of the matter was that the bitter feud that was playing out between Mitch and Mr. Raymond, so happened to intensify the ordeal. And with Melvin pulling away from one to join with the other—the one hated most by the former—this caused the situation to become far more uglier than thought. Even though the doors to Club Pressure hadn't opened as of yet, and Mitch hadn't paid any advance money to Melvin as his enemy Mr. Raymond was intent on doing, Melvin wasn't wrong with his decision. Therefore, Mitch hadn't lost anything, and no harm was caused on account of Melvin reneging, except to the pride and ego of Mitch maybe. And to add insult to injury, Melvin would still continue to have an affair with the man's daughter, a situation Mitch may not be able to tolerate.

Chapter 43

About two hours later, Melvin got into his truck and made the drive to the address Tisha had sent him. She owned an off-white, stucco brick home with pink trimming in the Little Haiti section of town. There was a bar gated fence to surround the home. The windows and doors were secured by bars as well. A two-car garage accompanied. He took notice of Tisha's white colored Range Rover parked inside. Melvin texted to notify her that he was out front her place. The sexy, dark-complexioned sweetheart of his appeared from the home and walked up to the Tahoe. Melvin lowered the window.

"Hey, baby," Tisha let out. The two kissed in the process.

"Hey. and I'm here," Melvin responded.

"I'm glad you were able to make it. Welcome to my house."

"It's a pleasure to be here. But ain't you gonna welcome me in or what?"

"Yeah, I am. But I wanted us to talk in complete privacy first. So, I'm about to hop in, okay?" she explained then strutted around to the passenger-side of the vehicle and entered.

"This is a nice home you have here, Tisha," he complimented.

"You like it?" was her response.

"I do."

"Well . . . if you're willing to do right by me and continue to treat me worthy like you have so far, you'll be the *man* over it, and have the leeway to run things how you see fit." Her declaration took Melvin by surprise.

"Oh, really!"

"Yes . . . really," she confirmed then eased closer to give him a kiss.

"But anyway . . . Please tell me that you haven't called or talked to your dad yet about the decision that I made?" he asked.

"Nope. And I assume you haven't either?"

"No . . . I haven't. I knew it was best to wait until the both of us were to meet and talk like we are now."

"Right. But if I must ask, what better offer did you receive to make you snub my father the way you did? And from who?"

"You want me to be all the way honest with you?" The way that Melvin worded this caused Tisha to brace herself in a way for what was to come.

"Yes . . . I do. I asked, didn't I?"

"How about, someone is willing to pay me $40,000 upfront, $90,000 a year, maybe more, and provide me a luxury car to go along with the money, because I'm gonna do some driving for him too."

"And you'll get all this to do exactly what type of work?" she wanted to know.

"To be one of two personal bodyguards," he replied.

"You still haven't said for who?"

"He's a high-profile guy who's now a politician."

"Be specific, baby," Tisha demanded.

"Mr. Raymond made me the offer to come work for him again. I couldn't say no to that," he finally revealed.

"Mr. Raymond made you the offer to come work for him again?!" Tisha retorted. She had a look of disgust now showing on her face. "Melvin, are you serious?! You mean to tell me that you'll go back to work for *that* dude again!

Ain't this a bitch!" she let out and slumped back unto the seat hard, crossing her arms in the process and grinding her teeth. After a pause, she raised up once more. "Melvin, how could you?!"

"It's simple to comprehend, sweetie. Mr. Raymond is willing to pay more money. Your dad didn't offer any money."

"So, my dad ain't offer you no money at all, you mean to tell me?"

"Nope. Not one red cent."

"But Melvin, you do know that my dad does plan to pay you and everybody else really good money to work for him, right? And just because he hasn't made you an offer doesn't mean that he's not willing to."

"Of course, I can understand that. And I do. But the bottom line is that, Mister Raymond, is gonna cut a check tomorrow at the time that we meet. And from there, we're gonna be on our way to bigger and better dealings. Besides, I'm thinking in the same way that Mr. Ray is thinking."

"And how is that?"

"I wasn't really looking to get back into the night club thing no way. Mister Raymond made a lot of sense to me when we talked along those lines. And who's better for me to take advice from other than him? At least that's how I see it. That's my take on it all."

Chapter 44

Tisha had gotten really quiet and began to contemplate on any way she could possibly think of to convince Melvin otherwise. She became vocal again. "Melvin, look at me," she said so to have solid eye contact and his total attention. It was necessary to not have either of the two to wonder for once.

"What's up?!" he stated, providing her what she'd asked.

"I already about know what my dad is gonna tell me to do once he learns of this. He's not gonna want me to have anything to do with you no more," she related. Tisha knew her father well enough to know that much.

"But I don't understand that part. Why would he make it his business to get mad at you for dealing with me, when what we have is totally unrelated to him and all he's trying to do? Make some sense of this for me please."

"Melvin. I don't know how to make it make sense for you. I'm just telling you. I know my father, and I know exactly what he's subject to say and might attempt to do."

"That doesn't mean you gotta go for it, Tisha. You're a grown woman. And in that regard, you gotta let him know where it is you stand."

"Yeah. You're right. I gotta let him know where I stand. No matter if he likes it or not. It's you who I want. It's you who I wanna be with. No matter what. I just don't wanna hear none of the bullshit I know he's gonna throw my way. But fuck it! It doesn't matter what he says. He won't know if I'm seeing you or not. But like I said, fuck it! It is what it is," Tisha stated. She leaned over to plant a passionate kiss on Melvin's neck.

The two began to tongue kiss at this point. Melvin's manhood rose instantly. His erection bulged aggressively through the fleece material sweatpants he had on. Tisha placed a hand under his shirt and began to caress on his chest while they continued to kiss. He let back the seat fully and took off his shirt. Her wet kisses continued from his neck, down to his chest, abs, and briefly halting at the waistline. He eased his pants and boxers down just past the knees. Tisha wasted no time to give the pleasure she knew would satisfy him. The latest album by Bryson Tiller, *True to Self*, played throughout the sound system. Track fifteen, *Set it Off*, beat from the speakers. A moment of desired intimacy was always a good way to make things right. At least for the time being.

—

The next day, Melvin texted Mitch and asked that he give him a call whenever his time permitted. He was situated at Traci's house for the time being. She was working as usual. Most days and nights, Melvin stayed over at her spot and not at his mother's, especially now behind the fact of Calvin and his sister appearing there looking to locate him.

Melvin wanted to have Calvin to continue in believing that he'd moved away once freed from prison, the story that his mother had already perpetrated for him. This was at least until Vick would be capable of having the hitters he was tied to track Calvin down and do the deed of killing the guy for them. The bottom line was that, Melvin needed Calvin to disappear. Forever. And each time he thought on how he'd missed on the guy's life, he wanted Calvin dead just that much more. As Vick had said, "the nigga was a nuisance," and the best way to deal with any and all nuisances was to eradicate them and leave it at that. There would be nothing more to report to the police or a jury by him.

Mitch eventually replied to the text by calling Melvin. His number appeared on the screen of the phone. The call was taken.

"Yo, Mitch! What's good, OG?! How you?" greeted Melvin.

"I'm well. What about you?" responded Mitch

"Everything kosher on my end."

"Good. But what's up? You wanted to speak with me, right?"

"Yeah, man. I do. And I'm aware that you're a man who don't like people to beat around the bush or procrastinate with what they have to say or do. So, I'mma just get straight to it," Melvin stated.

"Well, what you got? Get straight to it," Mitch urged him.

"About that agreement you and I had came to, the one where I said I will be a part of your security team for your new club when you open."

"Okay. What about it?"

"I'm not gonna be able to do it. I got a better offer from someone else." It took Melvin long enough, but he finally came on out with what he had to say.

"You not gonna be able to do it because you got a better offer from someone else?!" Mitch retorted. "What part of the game is this? And I guess that your word don't mean nothing to you, does it, Melvin?"

"Yeah, it does. But this is business, Mitch. Things are always subject to change, as you may already know. If anybody, you should be more aware of this than I am. And besides, I never signed any contract to make things official, nor did you put any upfront money in my pocket to truly convince me that being on your team, is where I wanna be," Melvin said to Mitch.

Chapter 45

"Melvin . . . look, I'm a product of the old school, homeboy. We *real niggaz* from the golden era, tend to take a man on the strength of his word when it comes to agreeing on a deal. This was something that you did, wasn't it? Gave me your word?" Mitch put his words in such a way to have Melvin clearly understand what he was getting at.

"I understand all of that, Mitch. Trust me, I do. But as I said, someone else made me a better offer. And you and I never agreed by way of a contract, which I have come to learn that this route is the best one to take when it comes to business. It's not personal," Melvin responded.

"You know what, Melvin . . . You a funny dude, you know that, brah?! I don't think you were able to really comprehend and process what was really going on at the time we talked. You didn't grasp my intent. There was a reason why I had you to meet up with me and we discussed *all* that we had," Mitch said with a serious tone to his voice.

"Maybe I'll understand it better if you just make it plain for me," responded Melvin.

"Look, man, okay. If you must know, I gave you my daughter. I allowed whatever it is you and her got going on to continue. If I didn't like you or didn't have any intentions of putting you down on my team and seeing to it that you prosper, I would've shut things down. And just so you'll know, I been knew that Tisha had a thing for you. And I want her to be happy because she deserves to be. That's why I told you that I know my daughter. Does that make sense to you now? Do you finally get it?"

"Everything that you saying makes sense to me, Mitch. But here's the deal. And I'm not trying to sound arrogant or conceited by stating the facts for you. And don't take what I'm about to say as a show of disrespect. But Tisha—your beloved daughter—was the one who chose me. I didn't choose her. So, regardless of if you are cool with *whatever* she and I got going on or not, Tisha is still gonna like me and deal with the man I am, who she chose to have in her life to be with. No matter what *Daddy* approves of or doesn't."

At the same time that Melvin was relating how he felt about everything that surrounded him and Tisha's affair, the thought passed through his mind of the sensational blow job that she'd given him just the day before. He was tempted to tell this to Mitch but didn't want to make an already bad sense of understanding between the two any worse. Melvin continued.

"That's one part of what I'm saying. The other is the offer I was made by someone else. I'll begin work and will be paid a nice amount of bread this week. There's no need for me to wait on work as I will be if I stayed in the agreement with you. My former boss, who is also the new boss—Mister Raymond Eugene Stephens—was the one who brought me back in and cut me a big boy check to go along with that like a—"

"Raymond!" Mitch cut in to retort. "Raymond!"

"Yeah . . . my boss. Mister Raymond Eugene Stephens. He's the man who made me a better offer and paid more dough. And I'll be one of his personal bodyguards. Not one of many bouncers at a *shaky-booty* club, you dig?"

"Nigga! I see now. You been down with that snake muthafucka all along, ain't you?" Mitch spat.

"Nah, I ain't. Not until the other day when I got a call from him when he reached out to me about the position. But

I see now where we going with this shit," Melvin responded. He detected hostility in the voice of Mitch.

"Melvin . . . truth be told, you not right, my guy. You try to appear as hardcore and real, but all you are is a grimy cutthroat nigga! I thought you were better than this. But I see now that some of the bullshit that Ray-Ray got going on with him done rubbed off on you."

"I'll take that with a grain of salt, Mitch, and continue to move forward."

"So, what you mention to that nigga about the agreement me and you had, if I may ask?"

"I told him about the proposal you flung at me. He offered to up that. And did," Melvin stated.

"You know what? I think I done heard enough of this shit! You be sure to stay away from my muthafuckin' daughter, nigga! I'll hate to be made aware that you didn't! Real talk!" Mitch stated then killed the connection on the call.

Melvin knew then without a doubt that Mitch was in the process of immediately calling Tisha and ordering her to not have any more to do with him. He had nothing to worry over in that regard. There wasn't a doubt that Tisha would soon thereafter call him to relate exactly what her father had said today and/or the threats that he'd made in the process. Tisha belonged to Melvin, and there wasn't shit Mitch was able to do about it. Nothing at all.

Chapter 46

Days Later . . .

Melvin received the text message from Mr. Raymond that he'd long awaited. There were only specific instructions for him to call at a certain time—at seven P.M. A mental note was made, and the alarm on the phone was set. Hours later, the time was at hand.

"This is Ray here!" he answered.

"Mister Ray! How you doing, man?" responded Melvin.

"I'm blessed, my guy. Just living and enjoying life and coming to realize the majesty of God's greater plan and preordained destiny that he has in place for me. What about you?"

"Oh, me . . . I'm well, Mister Ray. I just don't know how to thank you nearly enough for the opportunity that you have provided me with yet again. I appreciate everything about working for you. I really do, Mister Ray."

"That's good to know, Melvin. That's really good to know. And you're welcome. You are more than welcome. But on another note . . . did you tell Mitch to keep his offer?" Mr. Raymond asked. He had a bit of humor to his tone.

"Actually . . . I did. He wasn't too happy about it though. Dude sounded like if he was able to get his hands on me, he would indeed kill my ass, Mister Ray," Melvin returned the humor. "But question . . . why does dude seem so bitter toward you? I had thought that you two was like brothers," Melvin said.

"We were at one period in life. But Mitch is a miserable dude, Melvin. Miserable, I tell you. And as I've said, Mitch had began trying to do too much on me. He was attempting to be the boss. So, I let him have it. I gave him his money back and went on about my business, my brother. What did he have to say when you mentioned my name?"

"His words are not even worthy of repeating, Mister Ray. It would be an insult for me to do such a thing. But what I will say is this. He was sure to tell me to stop dealing with his daughter."

"He told you to stop dealing with his daughter? You and Tisha got something going on?" Mr. Raymond asked with a slight chuckle.

"So to speak," replied Melvin

"I knew you'd eventually end up with one of the girls from the club. Hell, we all did. Which isn't a bad thing. And Tisha is a good one though. She's a nice catch for you. I've never heard her name out there in any type of messed up way. She handles her business well."

"She's good. And we're good. I don't believe she'll go for *Daddy* trying to dictate to her who she can or who she can't be with. Tisha's with me now. And if Daddy don't like it, oh well," Melvin stated.

"I know that's right. But anyway, here is the business at hand between you and I. I'm in Palm Beach now at one of my little-known locations I like to lay low at. You're not busy in the next hour or so, are you?"

"Nah, I'm not. What's up?"

"I need for you to meet with me here today. I've got that money ready for you as well. And I wanna introduce you to my other guy. The intent is to implement our plan for how we are to move and go about doing things moving forward," Mr. Raymond related.

"That's a bet, Mr. Ray. I can make that happen."

"Good. I need for you to be sure to text me when you're halfway here. I'm gonna have someone meet you, and then you can follow them from there to here."

"Okay. I'm on my way in the next twenty minutes, Mister Ray."

"No doubt. I'm here."

The call concluded. Melvin took to task in preparing himself to meet with Mr. Raymond and company.

Chapter 47

Melvin made the drive from Miami to West Palm. Once there, Mr. Raymond instructed him to wait at a particular shopping plaza and that someone would arrive soon to escort him to the home where they were to meet. Melvin was eventually met by a female who was driving an Audi A4. The car was champagne colored and was one of the latest models. Mr. Raymond had mentioned to her what Melvin would be driving. She pulled closely to his SUV.

"Hi! I'm Camille," she greeted. Her skin complexion was a gorgeous pecan tan. She appeared to possess a nice figure from her face and neck. This was yet to be known. Melvin guessed that she was in her late forties to early fifties. She spoke further. "You're Melvin, right?"

"Indeed," he replied.

"Great! Raymond had me to meet you here. You are to follow me."

"Okay. I'm ready when you are."

They drove away at that point. Shortly thereafter, the two made it to an upscale gated community where it was apparent that rich, famous, and wealthy people lived. There were well maintained lawns, top dollar luxury automobiles dotted about here and there, and other articles of affluence. Melvin was convinced that there were more than a fair share of white people who lived there predominantly, who had both old and new money. All the roadways had near perfect paving, something an urbanized Black community had only dreamed of having. The entirety of the area screamed *well to do* at any new visitor immediately upon entry.

The female escort led the way to a driveway that belonged to a lavish two-story chateau styled manor that was off-white in color with powder blue trimming. Mr. Raymond's 600 series Mercedes Benz was observed by Melvin. It was parked in front of the garage. Camille exited the Audi. Melvin followed suit.

"Right this way, Melvin," she let out.

They reached the front door to the home. She unlocked the door, and they stepped inside. The house was a magnificent work of architectural designing. There was a high ceiling and an elegant chandelier in the center. Also, the place had a horseshoe stair casing that led to the second level. But to Melvin, one of the most extraordinary features of them all was the heavily glassed and fine polished grand piano that was situated in a corner of the living room to the left. It was solid white and matched well with the upholstery and decor that accentuated the haven.

Melvin followed Camille as she made her way to the right side of the house, down a short hallway, and to the front of a thick, wooden, double door. She twisted the handle and eased open one side, revealing a bar like setting. It was a positive energy type of area with a pleasant vibe, a cozy and welcoming atmosphere. The smooth grooves of Curtis Mayfield played at a modest volume. Melvin had a look inward and took sight of Mr. Raymond having a chat with a slim and fit guy at the bar. They conducted and carried themselves very suave and player-like. Mr. Raymond took notice of his presence and stood to his feet from the stool where he sat. Melvin approached and extended his hand to shake that of the boss.

"Hey, Mister Raymond! I'm pleased to be provided this opportunity to meet with you yet again," he greeted the politician in the making.

"My pleasure, Melvin. I'm glad to have you here," Mr. Raymond responded. "This here is Willie," he introduced and gestured with a wave of the hand from left to right. Willie got to his feet and prepared to shake Melvin's hand. "And Willie, meet Melvin, the young man I've been mentioning to you."

"What's good, Melvin? How you?" greeted Willie.

"I'm alright," he responded. The two shook hands.

"Well, Melvin, welcome to my secondary *casbah*," stated Mr. Raymond. He made a wide wave of the hand as if to say look at what I have here.

"Please . . . have a seat," he directed. Mr. Raymond had it really going on. So much so that the man's secondary pad was lavish, plush, and decked out to a high degree. And with this particular being declared number two, Melvin could only imagine what number one looked like. "This is my wine bar here. I am a collector. I also have a sizable stake in a winery. I'm looking to invest far much more into that at some point in the near future. If any thing, what would you like to sample? I have some of the best of everything." Mr. Raymond passed him a wine menu at that point.

"Hmm . . . let me see," Melvin responded and began to gaze over his options.

While in prison, he was an avid reader of the *Robb Report Magazine*. And with being a subscriber to RR, this prompted him to perform research into the wines and other alcoholic drinks and beverages that were featured. Therefore, he wasn't dumb to the brands that were presented or of the origins of those brands that existed around the world. So, when the question was posed by Mr. Raymond, Melvin was eager to inform a proper answer.

"Yes, Mister Ray. Let me have the Penfolds 2014 Grange. The Australian Red please," he requested.

Mr. Raymond jarred his head at what Melvin said. He was impressed. "You have nice taste I see," he complimented.

"Very much so, Mister Ray," Melvin responded.

Chapter 48

Mr. Raymond tapped a buzzer button that was situated atop the counter. Apparently, there was a somebody in the back whose attention was warranted because the next thing Melvin knew, a gorgeous, voluptuous, big booty, dark complexioned beauty dressed in designer labelled clothing came out. Her natural, thick, black hair was styled in a large afro puff pulled to the back and displayed radiant ripples of waves at the front and sides. She was evidently a barmaid who was hired by Mr. Raymond to serve.

"Melvin . . . meet Phaedra as well," he declared. Mr. Raymond then walked to the opposite side of the counter where she stood. He put an arm around her neck and displayed a sensational smile. Phaedra smiled at Melvin and extended a hand to shake his. He gently palmed hers to return the courteous mannerism.

"Hello, Phaedra! Nice to meet you too," Melvin said.

"And hello to you too, Melvin. Nice to meet you as well," the lovely lady said to the guest. She had a bit of an accent about her voice.

Mr. Raymond continued with a more formal introduction to who Phaedra was. "Miss Phaedra here . . . was born in America . . . but departed at a very early age with her musician father to live in Paris, France where she was raised. She was also educated and trained there in the art and craft of being a professional barmaid. Internships were granted for her to travel and work in various nations all about the

European union. She started a company—Phaedra Styles-Sartre Maidenette Services, LLC—and holds a license to do business here in the U.S. and abroad. How about that? Ain't that something?" he related and concluded with a smile.

"That's very impressive, I must say," stated Melvin. "Very impressive."

"What may I serve you, Melvin?" Phaedra asked.

"I'm having the Penfolds 2014 Grange." He pointed to his selection on the menu.

"I'll be more than pleased to serve you. You're one of the honored guests of Mister Raymond," she responded then sauntered to the back to retrieve Melvin a bottle of what he'd asked for.

"Mister Ray . . . you really got it going on, don't you?" Melvin complimented.

"No, Melvin. I'm not alone. It is *we* as a team that has it going on. Because when someone works for Raymond Eugene Stephens, you're family. You reap the benefit and pleasure of most of what I have when you have access to me the way that you two here have." He pointed back-and-forth from Willie to Melvin. "When I win, you win. And when I play. you play."

"You put that in a far better way than I did, Mister Ray," Melvin remarked. He smiled handsomely in knowing he'd made the best decision by rolling with Mr. Raymond and not Mitch. The man was looking to advance. With Mr. Raymond, he felt confident that he would.

"Okay, so now that you're here, let us get this part over and done with, shall we?" Mr. Raymond declared, producing a silver briefcase from behind the counter. He sat it atop and popped it open. This was the same money carrying item that he had with him at the club the night Melvin first met him. The chrome Colt .45 pistol with a pearl handle was inside, stacks of $100 bills, and a stack of documents. Apparently, this was a contract for Melvin to sign. "Melvin, I want you to thoroughly read over this before you sign and agree to anything, okay? This is simply for insurance purposes, a policy basically," Mr. Raymond said.

Melvin accepted the document and began to read over it. Indeed, the content thereof was related to insurance . . . Mr. Raymond's businesses and the cars that Melvin was to secure and drive. As for the *personal* aspects of their agreement, it was just that . . . *personal.* They required no contracts or stipulations. Melvin made a personal pledge to Mr. Raymond to stand guard and to serve and protect. No set of terms or conditions could be implemented regarding this. Melvin was very sure to voice this to Mr. Raymond at the completion of signing the contract, then he leaned forward to hug him, and Mr. Ray planted a kiss on his forehead. This was how true bosses complimented their loyalists who became made men. Mr. Raymond caused a feeling to arise in Melvin that made him believe that he was being taken in as a son to the man. This was because he'd never had anyone treat him in this manner before.

Chapter 49

"I love you, Melvin. Remember that always. Don't ever lose sight of that, okay?" he said to the protégé. "Now, here is the forty grand that I promised you," Mr. Raymond acknowledged then pitched over four $10,000 stacks. This was the most money that Melvin had ever made at any one time. He'd never been handed such a large amount of cash in one lump sum. "Also, here is an additional five thousand for you to play with. And since we got that part of the meeting complete, let's move along. Willie here is my absolute right-hand. He's the one I've kept by my side and out of the spotlight from the eyes of the public. You are to report directly to Willie on all matters. You got that?"

"Yes, sir, Mister Ray. I got that," Melvin responded.

"Good. And you get your instructions, your plans, your strategies, and all things security from Willie. He's your supervisor. It's imperative that you follow protocol. My life and the life of my family lies between the balance. That includes your life as well. What type of pistols you own? Although I'm aware you're a convicted felon, I'm sure you still carry something. If push ever comes to shove, I'll be able to get you out of any possession of firearms charges," Mr. Raymond stated.

"I've got what it takes. My P90 here," Melvin let out then placed the high-powered firearm on the counter after retrieving it from along his waistline, "and my .44 Bulldog to go along with it." He reached low to his ankle and brought out the mini crowd mover from the holster strapped there. This was set atop the counter as well.

"Nice choice of pieces you got there, Melvin," complimented Willie.

"More than likely, tomorrow, you and Willie here can get together and go over the vision and training on how you two are to coordinate with one another. He'll run down to you the codes, the signs, and the language for you to follow. Keep in mind it's only you and him for the time being. At least until the moment is ripe to move on to bigger and better things. But tonight, we drink, and we celebrate," Mr. Raymond announced. He hit the buzzer again for Phaedra to know that no more privacy was needed, and it was okay to return now with the bottle of wine Melvin had requested. She brought out glasses, a platter, and the necessary items to make cocktails. Mr. Raymond pulled out his cell phone and texted someone. It was Camille who he contacted. She sashayed through the doorway shortly thereafter and made her way to the bar to sip and chat with them.

Mr. Raymond made Melvin aware that Camille was, indeed, one of his most prized possessions. She was definitely not a bad looking woman for her age on any level. Ms. Camille stood at 5 foot 6, slim in the frame, had a low, natural, hair cut style, an immaculate texture of light brown, unblemished, unwrinkled skin. There were no marks or any signs of aging. Her face was oval-shaped. There was a slightly narrow, pointed nose that had a cuteness about it. Those greenish brown eyes she possessed revealed that there was a degree of creole in the mix of her DNA.

Mr. Raymond had more to add on regarding matters of security. "Oh, yeah, Melvin, from time to time, you and Willie will alternate on holding security detail post for Camille as well," he said as Camille eased closer to stand between his legs as he sat atop the stool again. They kissed. She produced a smile and drank on her cocktail that Phaedra had prepared for her. There was an olive in it. A toothpick was pierced down the center.

"I have no problem with that, Mister Ray," Melvin responded.

"The time to hold detail for her would be especially so whenever she's to travel to Miami. I want my sweetheart here to know that I have hired the best people to protect her. There are many sick and sadistic fools out there that are hellbent on trying to rob and extort anyone that they can for whatever they could. And Camille here, has a little dweeb down there at the house, who's become prone to stalking her. He's subject to causing problems. We'll make you more aware of him when the proper time to do so comes. But for right now, we're not gonna mention anything more about that clown. He's totally irrelevant by any configurations," Mr. Raymond stated. "But anyway, we're about thirty months out from the mayoral election, and I absolutely wanna have everything precise and on point leading into the race. My darling Camille here," he let out and hugged her tighter around the waist, "will certainly have the majority of her high-profile clients that bought property and homes through her real estate firm cast a ballot with my name on it and vote me into office. Also, once you get your money up, Melvin, my Camille shall be able to assist you with buying a nice home. As I've said, real estate is her area," Mr. Raymond informed Melvin.

Chapter 50

"Miss Camille, you're a very professionally oriented woman, I must say," Melvin complimented.

"Well, thank you, Melvin. That's nice of you to say." A smile appeared on her face as she accepted his kind words.

"Also, you have the looks, manners, and the etiquette of a woman who belongs between the pages of the business magazine, *Savoy*. Are you familiar with that particular publication?"

"Why yes . . . I am. I'm a subscriber to it. And what do you know about *Savoy*?" she asked curiously. Her smile at him continued.

"I'm a well read and thoroughly informed man, Miss Camille. I was sure to take advantage of the opportunity to become enlightened while repaying my debt to society. The time allotted to me made this possible," he related.

"Oh! Really? Well . . . that was indeed a good thing . . . to grab hold of the opportunity to learn."

Mr. Raymond then chimed in. "Yeah, sweetie . . . Melvin served almost two decades in federal prison. I was the first person to provide him a legit job when he got free. He's a reformed man without a doubt and was very much deserving of a second chance," he stated.

"Oh, wow! That's great. That's so great. Keep up the good work, Melvin. There's no limit to how far you can go in life," Camille said.

"Ain't that the truth? You're absolutely right about that," replied Melvin.

The five of them continued to lounge around, groove to the music, drink on wine and cocktails, and enjoy the company and conversation of one another. Melvin was provided the boost of confidence by Mr. Raymond he'd long sought to have. He was now in a good position next to a good man, and $45K richer. The $90,000 he was assured he'd make would most likely come long before a full year's worth of work was to be completed. Not to mention the fact that this was the line of work that he'd always wanted to perform. There wasn't any way he could lose or go wrong on this particular path to prosperity that was laid open for him. He was set up to win. He was destined to win. Period.

Chapter 51

Days Later . . .

The two-vehicle caravan of SUVs made it to the north in twenty-three hours from Miami following a pickup in Valdosta and Atlanta, Georgia. Vick and Melvin rode in the front with certain parts of all the guns in tow that they were transporting. They travelled in Melvin's Tahoe. Vick's other two guys, Nard and Danny, tagged along behind in Nard's Yukon Denali with a second portion of the firearms. Early on in Vick's gun trafficking career, he'd learned a trick or two about a particular way to avoid charges from the transporting of these weapons. In any situation where a cache of stolen guns were moved from one location to another—or in their case from one state to another—it was a must to break down the guns to two or three different pieces. For example, they removed all the top slides from every automatic pistol they had, the roulette barrels from all the revolvers were removed, and the clips and firing mechanisms were taken away from all the rifles.

Therefore, by disassembling the guns, this made them incomplete by definition as a firing weapon, and no charge of trafficking a firearm could be pinned upon them, no charges at all for that matter being that only pieces of guns were in one vehicle and pieces existed in the other. There was no law to constitute this.

It had been a long time since Melvin had journeyed to the north to do business by selling guns. And similar to Miami for him, nothing held a resemblance of what it used to be in these northern cities he'd once visited. There had been a far more radical transformation that took place there than in Dade County, but one thing that Melvin became aware of that hadn't changed was the cold weather that the north welcomed in each fall and winter. It was the last week of November that followed the Thanksgiving holiday, and it had been a rainy two days leading to this particular Friday that they'd arrived. The blistering cold seemed to be setting in early.

The first stop they made was in the Badlands, a section of North Philly. Melvin remembered some of those old haunts from times past, around the Erie Avenue and Germantown Avenue areas. Vick and a guy by the name of A.R. Harold had a business deal on a few pieces. Several actually. Harold was the leader of a street squad that controlled a particular turf in the surroundings. They ran things in their part of town. Those dudes held it down. Nobody was fucking with them when it came to trying to overthrow the operation they had in progress. And now that they were being provided additional fire power to safeguard what they owned, their security wouldn't suffer any type of breach.

The next stop for Vick, Melvin, and the other two was across the Benjamin Franklin bridge to Camden, New Jersey on 28th and 32nd Streets. Those dudes over in that town were a bunch of reckless, wild motherfuckers. A gangster by the name of Murder Mo, short for Mozique, had a small-scale operation going that possessed large scale tendencies. They seemed to be tested every day by competing groups and rivals on the 28th Street strip. Murder Mo was looking to bring all the tough guy shit others presented to an end. He'd already lost a couple of soldiers in various gun battles they'd had and wasn't looking to lose more. It was necessary to sling iron and spit slugs at the opposition to let them know that they meant business as well.

On 32nd Street, a cat named Maino was the big dawg on the block with the rank and the clout. He led the "wrecking crew". They were structured and trained to go.

The crew finally got out of Camden once the delivery was made, and the deals were sealed. With Vick doing the driving, he led the way up the New Jersey Turnpike, enroute to the Big Apple. He'd taken the same route so many times in the past that it became a familiar occurrence. They got off the expressway at Exit 16-E and headed toward the Lincoln Tunnel. Once through this underwater roadway, they got on 43rd Street, which took them to the New York convention center. You were only able to go right or left. They banged a left and were taken to the small Navy Yard that existed there. Vick turned right onto the Hudson River expressway and took the route uptown to the exit at 125th Street. He hooked a left on Broadway and journeyed up to 145th Street. After taking a right, they passed Amsterdam and went to St. Nicholas Avenue. Their trip came to an end at an apartment building in the "Sugar Hill" neighborhood. The night sky had set in. They got out. Every one of them were tired as shit. Rest was needed.

Chapter 52

Apparently, this had to be the spot where Vick's girl, Sakinah, lived. They removed the remainder of gun pieces from both trucks and made their way up the steep flight of stairs. Vick pulled out a key to the place and opened the door.

"Welcome to my Sugar Hill spot, fellas!" he let out with a huge smile.

Nard and Danny sat down the two large duffle bags that they carried then dapped up Vick and Melvin.

"Yo, we out, my niggaz," stated Nard. They were eager to get to a hotel for food, a shower, and rest before they were to head back down south in the next day or so.

"Word!" Vick responded then pulled out a few stacks of cash to pay them for their work. "Here y'all go. And y'all be safe on the ride home. But don't get lost in New York before you go because I'm sure y'all about to do a little shopping and touring while you're here for the next couple of days."

"You got to know that's what the plan is, bruh," said Danny. He was excited about being in the fashion capital of the world. The two then left. Vick and his cousin were to themselves yet again.

"Sakinah at work right now. She'll be home shortly, around ten-thirty," Vick related as he withdrew one of the three phones he had and began to text on it. More than likely, it was to Sakinah to let her know that they were there. "She's got a job doing hospice work for terminally ill elderly people," Vick mentioned.

"Oh, okay. That's what's up. And I hope she's got a sister, a cousin, or some homegirl chick I can get to know while I'm here these next two weeks," Melvin stated.

"She does.".

"Oh, word."

"Word, fam. And you should already know by now that I wasn't gonna bring you all the way up here and not establish a way for you to hook up with a female to occupy your time," said Vick.

"I know that to be the truth, fam. That's what the fuck I'm talking about," Melvin responded and began to briefly unpack their belongings.

—

Roughly one hour later, in came Vick's girl, Sakinah, to greet them on their visit. She stood at five-foot six inches in height. She was slim with a small waistline and flat mid-section, and she had an attractive figure. She had a shapely body, a round, plump butt, and was pigeon-toed and bow-legged. The particular features of her legs elevated her physical appearance to a level of exoticism. The way that Sakinah walked would have you to believe that she was the actress, Nia Long. Her skin complexion was that of hazelnut, creamy and smooth beyond the natural texture. Her head was wrapped in a black garment, so her hair wasn't readily visible. And she wore a thick Colombia coat to protect her from the cold weather that dominated.

"Peace and love, my queen!" Vick greeted with a smile. She approached him. They hugged and kissed before she could offer a reply.

"Peace and love, my king! How you be, Lord?" she responded with a gracious greeting of her own.

Melvin was made aware at that point that Sakinah was a woman who possessed sound knowledge of self in being good natured and Afrocentric. She smiled blissfully at Vick's presence. Those full, glossy lips of hers were on full display. She was bright eyed with delight. Her and Vick gazed at one another deeply as they continued to embrace.

"Sakinah, this is my cousin, Melvin, here. He's the one that I mentioned would be coming along with me," Vick said to her to make her aware.

"Hi, Melvin!" she greeted. "How are you?"

"I'm well, miss lady. My cousin, Vick, has shared so many wonderful things about you. He says that you are a life changing mate of his," Melvin let out.

"Oh, wow!" She glowed with admiration as she took a glance at Vick. They exchanged smiles once more. "Did he really say that? Or are you attempting to coerce us into getting married faster?"

"Don't feed off none of that stuff Melvin's saying to you, sweetheart. He's making that stuff up," Vick joked as he began to walk toward the kitchen to get them something more to drink.

Chapter 53

Melvin continued to sit on the couch and watch the basketball game that was on. The New York Knicks were playing Melvin's favorite team, the hometown Miami Heat. Vick returned with two bottles of Gatorade. He handed one to his cousin and then made his way to the bedroom to be with Sakinah. The green light was already given to Melvin to make himself at home. That was exactly what he'd done. He went to take a shower. Once complete, he made his way to the kitchen to fix something to eat. Upon opening the door to the refrigerator, he discovered nothing but whole foods and vegan related products. Melvin wasn't a huge meat eater anu way, but he did enjoy a nice piece of chicken from Popeyes or Church's every now and again.

He settled for fruit, two bagels, and a nice cup of coffee. Once returning to his seat on the couch, he went back-and-forth between ESPN, CNN, FOX NEWS, and VICELAND. The basketball game had ended. As usual, the Knicks got the shit beat out of them. And for the Knicks fan who'd heckled the Knicks owner, James Dolan, he was absolutely correct with his criticism of Dolan and suggesting that he should sell the team. The Knicks were pathetic in every aspect of the word.

Vick nor Sakinah never returned from the room that night. Melvin pulled out his cell phone and began to interact on social media to the point of where he'd dozed off to sleep himself. When he awoke the next morning on the couch, he took notice of Vick and his New York sweetheart both in the kitchen. Vick found himself seated at the table, reading a copy of the *Wall Street Journal*, and Sakinah was preparing breakfast for them all.

"Rise and shine, Melly-Mel," he said to Melvin.

"I'm up. . . I'm up, fam. What's good?" Melvin responded. He went to his tote bag to get his toothbrush and toothpaste. He made his way to the bathroom to take care of his hygiene. Once done, Melvin returned to their presence. He took a seat at the table and began to eat along with Vick as Sakinah remained standing and talking with them.

"So, Melvin, this your first time in New York?" Sakinah asked in her heavily proper accent.

"Nah. I've been up through here before. Not necessarily Harlem per se but Brooklyn," Melvin responded.

"Oh. okay. You are familiar with the Big Apple then, huh?"

"So-so."

Melvin was able to gain a good look at Sakinah this morning. She didn't have on a head wrap or thick clothing to battle the cold weather. She had thin, twisted, neat dreadlocks that flowed down to her shoulders. The tips to them were dyed blonde and what remained was all black. There were none that were gray or white. Her face glowed illustriously. The choice of clothing that she had on wasn't so revealing since she maintained a high level of respect for herself and a high level of respect for the man who was in her life, Vick.

"Sakinah. . . Vick made me aware of you and all to expect. That's the reason why I find myself speaking so loosely with you like I know you," Melvin said to her.

"I understand. You good."

"Yeah, you good, cuz. Sakinah is family to you now. Y'all gotta get to know of one another. And how you do that is through conversation, right?" Vick let out.

"Absolutely. Ain't no doubt about that. But anyway, look, what lifestyle or particular school of thought do you adhere to, Sakinah, if you don't mind me asking? I'm curious to know since Vick has said that you're more qualified to answer that than he is," Melvin said.

"My way of life? I'm *Earth-Body*, a member of the Nation of Gods and Earths. You heard of us before?"

"Of course, I have. I was around a lot of those cats when I was in the pen."

"In the pen?!" Sakinah retorted.

"Sweetie, this the cousin who I told you about that's like a brother to me, the one who was on his way home when we met. Remember?" Vick chimed in to say.

"Oh, yeah, I do. So, this is him, right?"

"Yes. He's the one," Vick confirmed.

Sakinah smiled behind Vick's words and continued to chat further with Melvin. "But yeah, I'm with NGE. I also ascribe to a Bohemian lifestyle as a way to express myself through my artistic talents that I have."

"Artistic talents? Such as?" Melvin desired to know.

"Artistic talents such as. . . I write. . . and I do art. I can paint and draw my ass off," she boasted in a confident manner. With a wave of her hand, she gestured for Melvin to have a look around him at a demonstration of her work on display in her living room.

He did so. "You painted all of these portraits?"

"The majority of it, I did," she replied.

Chapter 54

"Wow! That's a beautiful thing," Melvin complimented and continued to rove his head in awe at the creation he looked on at. "But in moving forward, I'm curious to know what's your outlook on life for us Black men in your art and in the way we could be elevated through that medium? My reason for asking is because I see and also know what type of effect you have upon my people, and I think what you have to offer may rub off on other Black women in a positive way," Melvin stated. He was really interested in hearing her expound in her own artistic and stylistic way like the adherents of the NGE do. They had a captivating lingo in how they verbally appealed with their word play.

"Well, first and foremost, everything begins and ends with the individual. In order for the Black man to become God, he has to first know God. And that is to say this is a self-realizing process for he who exists within that is greater than thine-self. . . is the most high. The mind that rules the body serves as the master which dictates to the slave. But. . . we can build more on all this at a later time and date. I know that my babe here has business to handle. And I do so as well. It's one of my days off, and there's no need to ask me. Vick has already made your desires known to me. I've got a cousin that's single, and I'm sure she wouldn't mind having herself a down south dude. So, with that being said, I got you, Melvin," Sakinah said, kissed Vick once more, and made her way to the bedroom, leaving the guys to themselves to enjoy the meal she prepared.

Vick became vocal again. "So, yeah, cuz, we'll meet up with Fat Tony later this evening to deliver his order, get our bread, and then meet up with him again in the A.M. to catch one of those dope dog fighting events that he's known for hosting. Like I mentioned to you before, them niggaz be betting some serious money at those matches. And fam, when I say some serious paper, I mean some serious paper. Paper like three, four, or even five hundred dollars, my nigga! Me personally. . . I simply love the entire sport of it all," proclaimed Vick. He seemed to be full of passion and enthusiasm.

"I'm already knowing, fam. I can tell by the way you're speaking on it that the thrill of it all has to be an addictive thing. You may be able to convince me to fall in love with that shit the same way that you have," Melvin responded.

"Trust me, cuz. . . you're subject to fall in love with this shit after only one event."

"Who knows? I just may."

Chapter 55

With their work complete and their touring of New York City done, Nard and Danny had already hit the road and made their way back to Miami. They'd performed in all they were paid to do. And the primary reason why Vick and Melvin were intent on staying there longer was because Vick desired to spend additional time with Sakinah, go shopping, continue to network and become more acquainted with those dudes there who were getting real money in the underworld and living good, and to further come to know the city in the event that he was to decide to move there from Miami.

Vick wanted his respect in the locale the same as Fat Tony and the other Big Willies he did business with. Through the years that Melvin was away, Vick had really gotten on top of his game. Melvin took note of his rise to power first-hand now and admired how he conducted and carried himself. Vick was super smooth with his method of safekeeping. He had a large stash of cash at Sakinah's house. And Sakinah, in return, had done a very good job of keeping the money secured and portions thereof properly invested in the right areas.

Fat Tony put off the meeting and business arrangement with Vick until the Sunday of the weekend which was upon them. He had a family emergency to deal with. But now, the day was at hand, and the two cousins made their way to meet Fat Tony. He didn't live too far from where Sakinah did. East Harlem was his stomping ground.

Melvin found himself a nervous wreck behind them transporting all those pistols and rifles in this particular city that possessed a heavy police presence no matter if the weapons were still broken down to pieces or not. Once arriving at the apartment building where Tony lived, the two hiked the flight of stairs to get to the top floor. Melvin had no idea on what to be more afraid of—the NYPD performing a raid on a potentially hot rest haven or those New York niggaz kicking in the door to rob them for all they had, rather by set-up on Tony 's behalf, or, with him as a target. Vick had spoken to him prior to leaving Sakinah's spot to let him know that they were on the way. Fat Tony was expecting them.

Vick knocked on the door to Tony 's pad. There was a tall, fat, husky dude who appeared.

"Yo, Vick! What's good, son? How you?" Fat Tony greeted.

"I'm good, Tony. How you been, my nigga?" Vick replied. The two dapped up one another. They embrace as well. "This my people here, Tony. His name Melvin, but everyone calls him Parlay," Vick introduced.

"What up, Parlay? I'm Tony, as you may know already. Good to meet you," Tony said to him while keeping solid eye contact. He dapped Melvin as well. They also embraced.

"I'm kosher, Tony. Nice to meet you too, bro," Melvin responded.

"Here are those pieces you ordered, big dawg," Vick declared then unzipped both duffle bags for Tony to examine. "And you already know we're gonna help you put each one back together before we leave you. Just like last time. The best way to avoid a gun charge is by doing them this way."

Fat Tony smiled behind Vick's remark. "You a smart dude, Vick. You're the only person I've ever dealt with for guns who had sense enough to know how to beat the cops in this game. I commend you on this," he complimented.

"I appreciate that, bro. I really do."

"No problem. But look . . . y'all take a seat for a minute," Tony urged them. "I'll be right back." He left the two in the living room and made his way to the back of the apartment.

Vick and Melvin sat on the couch. Roughly two minutes later, Tony returned with a tote bag that was loaded with money. He had everything sorted in $5,000 stacks. He then proceeded to count out the payment aloud in the presence of his guests. The total was $80,000.

"Here is the sixty to pay for everything now, the ten thousand I owe you, and another ten Gees in advance on the next order," Fat Tony stated.

"I love how you do business, big dawg," Vick let out with a smile. "It's always a pleasure doing so with you."

"Nah, dawg. I love how *you* do business, my G, and it's always a pleasure doing so with you," Fat Tony came back with. He and Vick smiled at one another, dapped up once more, and embraced to complete the deal. Melvin looked on at the smooth business transaction and was compelled to smile himself.

"Yo, you still hosting that dog show tomorrow?" asked Vick.

"Hell fuck yeah, my nigga!"

Vick brought out the passion of Fat Tony that he held inside regarding the world of Pitbulls.

"You got to know that, Vick! This is my life. I live for this shit, yo! I wish like hell I could've did it yesterday. But I had a serious situation to attend to with my grandmom. She had to be rushed to the hospital. But yeah, shit still gonna be on and poppin," Tony stated emphatically.

"That's good 'cause we'll be here in New York to see it," Vick responded.

"For sho. I'll text you and send photos to showcase the gladiators that's supposed to do battle."

"That's a bet. But look. . . let me and fam get up outta here so you can handle your business, and we can go and handle ours. You need our help putting those bangers back together again, or you good to go?"

"I'm good to go. I got it. Remember, I'm a vet too," Fat Tony declared with a smile.

Vick and Melvin admired the level of confidence that was put on display. They all dapped up and embraced one last time before the boys from down south were to depart the premises. "We'll see you tomorrow, Tony."

"No doubt."

The duo made their way back to Sakinah's place to put away the money. Once there, they double counted and were sure to check to be sure there wasn't any counterfeit bills in the mix. The streets were vicious, and no one could be trusted who was a product thereof.

Everything checked out. Fat Tony proved authentic. Vick took the bread to the bedroom. Sakinah was there. He returned to the living room and gave Melvin an additional $15,000. The man was determined to assist his people with getting back on his feet financially.

"More where this came from as we move forward, fam," stated Vick. "And it'll definitely get greater later. Just continue to be patient."

Melvin graciously accepted the money. He had no complaints about anything. The man simply continued to go with the flow and allowed his cousin to lead the way. His payment came to him by being the wingman throughout the operation of their journey to the north. This wasn't a bad position to play by any means.

Epilogue

Vick and Melvin rested up for the night and were again up early. The time was 8:30 A.M. "Yo, cuz, we gotta head back to see Fat Tony in the next hour or so. I'm anxious to see about those dog matches," Vick related to Melvin. Tony had sent those text messages and photos of the contenders who were on the schedule to fight. The time was also provided for when they needed to show if they were intent on being there.

Melvin brushed his teeth, washed his face, and ate the breakfast with Vick that was prepared for them by Sakinah. She'd taken off to work hours earlier. From that point, the two made their way back to Fat Tony's pad. Instead of going up the stairs, they descended downward to the basement of the building where there was a boxing ring sized pit for the dogs to fight in. Tony had a bleacher stand next to it. Roughly fifteen people were already on hand and ready for the entertainment to begin. There were isolated corners that had dogs situated in them, their handlers, and certain clothes from the kennel unit that the dog belonged to that they represented. The dogs all had on a muzzle to prevent any barking as they were being prepared to perform.

Fat Tony appeared to greet Vick and Melvin. "Man, Vick, I'm glad you and your people, Parlay here, were able to make it. I've got a show lined up for y'all today, my nigga. Two of my dogs gonna be getting busy! It's six matches on schedule. I'm running with that 'Nigerino' bloodline with one of my boys. And on the other, he's that Pat Patrick's Tombstone bloodline. It's about $400,000 that'll be put down on bets over the whole event. I've had my boys training for the past eight weeks for today, my nigga. And we ready to do something," Fat Tony said.

"You already know we with you, my nigga. So, let's get-get-get it!" responded Vick.

"I'm ready for it," Melvin chimed in to say.

Vick put up $10,000 on each of Tony 's dogs, and Melvin laid out $5,000 on each. The first two matches involved Tony 's two soldiers. They both won—in a convincing way as well. Vick and Melvin collected their earnings. Following on the advice of Tony in knowing the dogs and the owners who handled them, additional bets were made on the remaining four matches. They went five and one. The entire event lasted maybe seven hours. Tony had put on a really good show. Everyone who was there saluted him. And the truth be told, Melvin had no awareness of exactly how addictive that the sport could become. After one show, he was hooked. He wanted more.

To make matters more interesting for Melvin, he'd come to learn that the dog fighting game even went so far as to crown consecutively winning dogs the title of champion following three official wins and a grand champion following five official wins. Any losing dogs were subject to be eradicated by the owner through certain means if they didn't prove to be truly "game" over the inability to physically defeat the opposing dog.

Melvin fell in love with the sport so quickly that he went as far as to buy a female puppy from Fat Tony. He paid $3,500 for her. His new bitch belonged to that Nigerino bloodline Fat Tony bragged so heavy about. He named her *Coco K*, short for *Coco Kardashian*. He chose such a name because he held ambition to take over the game through her, by properly breeding, inbreeding, raising, and thoroughly training, much the same as Momma Kardashian had done with her girls, minus the inbreeding part.

The final few days of their week-long visit was upon them and their stay in New York City. On this particular day—a Wednesday—Vick and Melvin made a return to Sakinah's place following a day of shopping for street gear. They entered the apartment and took notice that she had company present with her. It was another female. The two favored one another in appearance. They shared the same set of eyes and also skin complexion. A couple of dreadlocks dangled from underneath the other female's head wrap she styled herself in.

———

This has to be the cousin of Sakinah's she mentioned before, Melvin thought

"Hey, babe!" greeted Vick to Sakinah. He approached her, and they hugged and shared a passionate kiss. "And what's good with you, Miss Yvette, aka 'True Queen Mecca'?" he stated to the female guest. It was obvious they were familiar with one another. "Yo, Melvin . . . this here is Sakinah's people she told you she'd introduce you to. And as you heard me say, her name is Yvette," Vick let out loudly and in a playful banter type of way. He smiled from ear to ear. He and the girl then exchanged a volley of playful punches.

"I know how to introduce myself, Vick. I don't need you to do that for me. I got it!" she responded to what Vick had initially done.

He turned away and headed to the kitchen. More than likely, it was for a bottle of Gatorade.

"I apologize for his rudeness," Yvette said to Melvin with a smile. She then extended her hand to shake his. He gently palmed it. The time to properly introduce herself was at hand. "I'm Yvette. I go by my righteous name as well. It's True Queen Mecca!"

"It's a pleasure to meet you, miss lady," Melvin proclaimed confidently. "As you know, I'm Melvin. But I go by Parlay too. Nice to meet you as well," he responded. His focus was transfixed on her beauty and luscious skin complexion. The glitz of her eyes appeared to change colors at various angles that the light reflected. Yvette took note of the captivation that he had of her eyes.

"They're real," she let out with a smile. "I don't do fake. Period. No contact lenses. No lipstick. No press on or glued nails. No make-up, weaves, wigs, or otherwise. I could never settle for being an artificially assembled female," she adamantly professed.

"I don't think I'd have you no other way than as you are. I absolutely love and adore a woman who's deeply grounded in the knowledge of who they are and her kind. I appreciate being intellectually stimulated, my dear," stated Melvin.

Sakinah was still there in their presence. She took note of the two getting acquainted. Yvette spoke out to her on Melvin's articulate prowess. "Ooh, Sakinah. He's a man who knows how to express himself too, I see. I think I like him already," she declared to her cousin.

Melvin took the opportunity to serenade her further and appeal to her "Asiatic Soul" with his depth in wordplay. His desire was to have her feel where he was coming from. Although he'd never professed it to Vick or Sakinah, dude had actually been a long student and devout adherent to the five percent lessons and doctrine. One particular tenant of the organization was that, "if something sounds right, then it could be reasoned with," so long as the evidence and the proof was there to support it. He based what more he had to say on this premise.

Vick and Sakinah left the two to talk more. They made their way to the bedroom. The plan was for the four of them to go out to eat later in the evening at one of Sakinah's favorite restaurants. It was a vegan spot. Melvin was the only one of the four who ate meat or consumed any animal byproducts. Nonetheless, he had no problem partaking in a meatless diet for one night. Who knew? He may begin to take a liking to it.

The way that Melvin began to perceive things, if Yvette continued to turn him on and impress him the way that she had, he would proceed on the course that he was and live up to the expectations of a special kind of man that she desired in her life. He could really get used to her—her petite frame, the bumblebee waistline, and the apple bottom having Bohemian bombshell that he had in her. He loved her style. He loved her finesse. He adored those elegant Pekingese facial features of "True Queen Mecca". She seemed to be a keeper.

As much as Sakinah and Yvette highly respected and valued simplicity over expensiveness or extravagance, they certainly had not refused the boys from taking them on a shopping spree in Midtown Manhattan at Saks Fifth Avenue and other high-end stores. Together, Vick and Melvin spent about $17,000 on the ladies and themselves.

They didn't mind showing love being that every penny that went toward catering to them had been won at the dog fighting event held by Fat Tony. Similar to Vick with Sakinah, Melvin looked to establish something in the future with Yvette—something for the long haul. They were both feeling one another. He desired to set up a structure in New York like Vick as the way that Vick maintained a second foundation there in the north was a wise move to make. Note was taken of this by Melvin of Vick's blueprint and play book. There was no way either of the two could lose or go wrong like this.

Once back at Sakinah's place, Melvin and Yvette exchanged information, hugs, and kisses, as they vowed to keep in touch until he was to return. At no time did he try to press her for sex or any other intimate activity. He wasn't up there for that. Business was the priority, although he happened to get lucky throughout the process. However, the next trip would be a combination of business and pleasure. He was destined to indulge in both.

As for the dog that Melvin bought from Fat Tony, she would be shipped to him by plane once back in Miami. All of the other business of the day was taken care of. Melvin and Vick were set to hit the road again in Melvin's Tahoe truck the next day at six P.M. and return home. A deep and thorough discussion was on the agenda to be had by the two during the travel.

—

Vick and Melvin would go on to speak over all that they'd brought to New York, all they sold in New York, on all they'd done while there, who they met, who purchased from them, and what was to be on the next trip. Little to their knowledge, the two had been severely compromised long in advance.

Trouble was on the horizon in a damaging way. Had Melvin truly known the person he was acquainted with, prior to simply taking up the suggestion to go out and buy the Tahoe he now owned, all because the person doing the suggesting, thought that such a vehicle would be a nice ride for him, the dire situation that was building against he and Vick, wouldn't now be so. But when the federal government wanted you, they'd go to great lengths to get you. This was what occurred, at the time when they planted the eavesdropping devices all throughout Melvin's Tahoe before he purchased it, then had their special agent, Ursula Corbin, aka Yolanda, convince him to buy the truck. There was nothing he or Vick could do to take back what had already been spoken by them and heard by the Feds. They now knew far too much.

To Be Continued . . .

COMING SOON IN THE SERIES

RELENTLESS GOON 3
Love & Gunplay
**OTHER BOOKS AVAILABLE BY THE AUTHOR
AND LDP**

BLOODLINE OF A SAVAGE
(A Bill Hilliard Trilogy)
BLOODLINE OF A SAVAGE 2
Revelations
BLOODLINE OF A SAVAGE 3
Wrath

THESE VICIOUS STREETS
Love & Money
THESE VICIOUS STREETS 2
Pressure
THESE VICIOUS STREETS 3
Wicked Ambitions

SAVAGE FAMILY EMPIRE
Money
SAVAGE FAMILY EMPIRE 2
Power
SAVAGE FAMILY EMPIRE 3
Respect

ABOUT THE AUTHOR

PRINCE A. TAUHID is a writer of gritty, raw, dark, and suspenseful contemporary urban/street crime fiction. The works of his embody American society and African American culture as is in the way that it is. Nothing less. Nothing more. The characters he creates are realistic in nature in all of their wiles and ways. The style of writing Prince has developed speaks for itself. You're drawn in the more and more you read until you're locked there with one way in and no way out. In a word to describe his skills within the craft, it's **LETHAL**.

Prince vehemently declares at every opportunity that, **"WRITING IS MY ONLY SALVATION!"** He stands firmly on business with this.

The works he's released thus far are the popular **BLOODLINE OF A SAVAGE** series (three instalments to date), **THESE VICIOUS STREETS** series (three instalments to date), **RELENTLESS GOON** series (three instalments to date), **NIGHTMARE**. and **THE REDEMPTION CHRONICLES** series to name a few. More captivating series are on the way.

Prince is currently hard at work on his next novel. In addition to the story you've just read here, look forward to new releases from him soon. Prince highly encourages feedback and engaging conversation about his books and the writing industry in general. You may contact him at the following:

PRINCE A. TAUHID #952058
MACON STATE PRISON
P.O. BOX 426
OGLETHORPE, GEORGIA 31068
iamprinceforever3000@gmail.com

The Pen Is Mightier Than The Pistol
EMBRACE WRITING!

Lock Down Publications and Ca$h Presents
Assisted Publishing Packages

Due to an increase in the price of services we have increased our prices. The prices below reflect the price increase as of 11/1/24.

BASIC PACKAGE	UPGRADED PACKAGE
$699	$1000
Editing	Typing
Cover Design	Editing
Formatting	Cover Design
	Formatting
	Upload eBooks to Amazon
	Upload Paperback to Amazon
ADVANCE PACKAGE	**LDP SUPREME PACKAGE**
$1,400	$1,700
Typing	Typing
Editing (line editing/content)	Editing (line editing/content)
Cover Design	Cover Design
Formatting	Formatting
Copyright Registration	Copyright Registration
Proofreading	Proofreading
Upload eBooks to Amazon	Set up Amazon Account
Upload Paperback to Amazon	Upload eBooks to Amazon
	Upload Paperback to Amazon
	Advertise on LDP's Amazon and Facebook Page

***Other services available upon request.
Additional charges may apply

Lock Down Publications
P.O. Box 944
Stockbridge, GA 30281-9998
Phone: 470 303-9761
Email: lockdownpublications@gmail.com

Submission Guideline

Submit the first three chapters of your completed manuscript to ldpsubmissions@gmail.com. In the subject line add **Your Book's Title**. The manuscript must be in a Word Doc file and sent as an attachment. Document should be in Times New Roman, double spaced, and in size 12 font. Also, provide your synopsis and full contact information. If sending multiple submissions, they must each be in a separate email.

Have a story but no way to send it electronically? You can still submit to LDP/Ca$h Presents. Send in the first three chapters, written or typed, of your completed manuscript to:

LDP: Submissions Dept
P.O. Box 944
Stockbridge, GA 30281-9998

DO NOT send original manuscript. Must be a duplicate. Provide your synopsis and a cover letter containing your full contact information.

Thanks for considering LDP and Ca$h Presents.

NEW RELEASES

BLOODLINE OF A SAVAGE 1,2&3
THESE VICIOUS STREETS 1,2&3
RELENTLESS GOON
RELENTLESS GOON 2
BY PRINCE A. TAUHID

THE BUTTERFLY MAFIA 1-3
BY FUMIYA PAYNE

A THUG'S STREET PRINCESS 1,2&3
BY MEESHA

CITY OF SMOKE 1& 2
BY MOLOTTI

STEPPERS 1,2&3
THE REAL BADDIES OF CHI-RAQ
BY KING RIO

THE LANE 1&2
BY KEN-KEN SPENCE

THUG OF SPADES 1,2&3
LOVE IN THE TRENCHES 2
CORNER BOY CHRONICLES
BY COREY ROBINSON

TIL DEATH 3
BY ARYANNA

THE BIRTH OF A GANGSTER 4
BY DELMONT PLAYER

RELENTLESS GOON 2 | PRINCE A. TAUHID

PRODUCT OF THE STREETS 1&2
BY DEMOND "MONEY" ANDERSON

NO TIME FOR ERROR
BY KEESE

MONEY HUNGRY DEMONS 1,2&3
BY TRANAY ADAMS

HUNGRY FOR MONEY 1&2
BY SLIMBOS

A THUGGISH PASSION
KILLAZ ON STANDBY 1&2
LAND OF DA HOOLIGANZ 1,2&3
FRESH OFF DA PORCH
BY IRA B.

COUNTDOWN OF A KILLA 1&2
GUNS DOWN, BOTTOMS UP 1&2
SEX, MURDA AND GOD
BY LO-LIFE

THE LEVEL UP 1&2
BY LUXURY KING

FO'EVA ROLLIN' 1&2
BY ASSA RAYMOND BAKER

HUB CITY MENACE 1&2
BY J. WHITE

KILLA CREW
DYING FOR LIKES
BY ARYANNA

IF YOU CROSS ME ONCE 6
ANGEL 5
By Anthony Fields

IMMA DIE BOUT MINE 5
By Aryanna

A THUGS STREET PRINCESS 3
EMBRACING THE LOVE OF A BOSS
By Meesha

PRODUCT OF THE STREETS 3
By Demond Money Anderson

STANDING ON HER BUSINESS
BY DG SANTANA

GET IT IN SLUGS 1&2
B. STALLS

CORNER BOYS 2
By Corey Robinson

THE MURDER QUEENS 6&7
By Michael Gallon

CITY OF SMOKE 3
By Molotti

CONFESSIONS OF A DOPEBOY
By Nicholas Lock

TENDER
BY KHUFU

THA TAKEOVER
By Keith Chandler

BETRAYAL OF A G 2
By Ray Vinci

CRIME BOSS 4
By Playa Ray

Coming Soon from Lock Down Publications/Ca$h Presents

RAN OFF ON THE PLUG 2 by **PAPER BOI RARI**
STREET REDEMPTION by **TONY DANIELS**
SAVAGE FAMILY EMPIRE by **PRINCE TAUHID**
BAD BITCHES WIT' GUNZ by **DIESEL**
THE SINGLE LADIES by **DIESEL**
COKE BY THE TRUCKLOAD by **DIESEL**
PROBLEM SOLVED by **DIESEL**
TIPPIN' THE SCALES by **DIESEL**
OPPS CRY TOO by **SAYNOMORE**
A GANGSTA'S KARMA by **FLAME**

AVAILABLE NOW

RESTRAINING ORDER 1 & 2
By **CA$H & Coffee**

LOVE KNOWS NO BOUNDARIES 1-3
By **Coffee**

RAISED AS A GOON I, II, III & IV
BRED BY THE SLUMS I, II, III
BLAST FOR ME I & II
ROTTEN TO THE CORE I II III
A BRONX TALE I, II, III
DUFFLE BAG CARTEL I II III IV V VI
HEARTLESS GOON I II III IV V
A SAVAGE DOPEBOY I II
DRUG LORDS I II III
CUTTHROAT MAFIA I II
KING OF THE TRENCHES
By **Ghost**

LAY IT DOWN I & II
LAST OF A DYING BREED I II
BLOOD STAINS OF A SHOTTA I & II III
By **Jamaica**

LOYAL TO THE GAME I II III
LIFE OF SIN I, II III
By **TJ & Jelissa**

IF LOVING HIM IS WRONG…I & II
LOVE ME EVEN WHEN IT HURTS I II III
By **Jelissa**

PUSH IT TO THE LIMIT
By **Bre' Hayes**

BLOODY COMMAS I & II
SKI MASK CARTEL I, II & III
KING OF NEW YORK I II, III IV V
RISE TO POWER I II III
COKE KINGS I II III IV V
BORN HEARTLESS I II III IV
KING OF THE TRAP I II
By **T.J. Edwards**

WHEN THE STREETS CLAP BACK I & II III
THE HEART OF A SAVAGE I II III IV
MONEY MAFIA I II
LOYAL TO THE SOIL I II III
By **Jibril Williams**

A DISTINGUISHED THUG STOLE MY HEART I - III
LOVE SHOULDN'T HURT I II III IV
RENEGADE BOYS 1-4
PAID IN KARMA 1-3
SAVAGE STORMS 1-3
AN UNFORESEEN LOVE 1-3
BABY, I'M WINTERTIME COLD 1-3
A THUG'S STREET PRINCESS 1&2
By **Meesha**

CUM FOR ME 1-8
An LDP Erotica Collaboration

BLOOD OF A BOSS 1-5
SHADOWS OF THE GAME
TRAP BASTARD
By **Askari**

A GANGSTER'S CODE 1-3
A GANGSTER'S SYN 1-3
THE SAVAGE LIFE 1-3
CHAINED TO THE STREETS 1-3
BLOOD ON THE MONEY 1-3
A GANGSTA'S PAIN 1-3
BEAUTIFUL LIES AND UGLY TRUTHS
CHURCH IN THESE STREETS
By **J-Blunt**

THE STREETS BLEED MURDER 1-3
THE HEART OF A GANGSTA 1-3
By **Jerry Jackson**

WHEN A GOOD GIRL GOES BAD
By **Adrienne**

THE COST OF LOYALTY 1-3
By **Kweli**

BRIDE OF A HUSTLA 1-3
THE FETTI GIRLS 1-3
CORRUPTED BY A GANGSTA 1-4
BLINDED BY HIS LOVE
THE PRICE YOU PAY FOR LOVE 1-3
DOPE GIRL MAGIC 1-3
By **Destiny Skai**

A KINGPIN'S AMBITION
A KINGPIN'S AMBITION II
I MURDER FOR THE DOUGH
By **Ambitious**

A DOPEBOY'S PRAYER
By **Eddie "Wolf" Lee**

TRUE SAVAGE 1-7
DOPE BOY MAGIC 1-3
MIDNIGHT CARTEL 1-3
CITY OF KINGZ 1&2
NIGHTMARE ON SILENT AVE
THE PLUG OF LIL MEXICO 1&2
CLASSIC CITY
By **Chris Green**

LOVE & CHASIN' PAPER
By **Qay Crockett**

THE KING CARTEL 1-3
By **Frank Gresham**

THESE NIGGAS AIN'T LOYAL 1-3
By **Nikki Tee**

GANGSTA SHYT 1-3
By **CATO**

THE ULTIMATE BETRAYAL
By **Phoenix**

BOSS'N UP 1-3
By **Royal Nicole**

I LOVE YOU TO DEATH
By **Destiny J**

BROOKLYN HUSTLAZ
By **Boogsy Morina**

GANGSTA CITY
By **Teddy Duke**

TO DIE IN VAIN
SINS OF A HUSTLA
By **ASAD**

I RIDE FOR MY HITTA
I STILL RIDE FOR MY HITTA
By **Misty Holt**

A GANGSTER'S REVENGE 1-4
THE BOSS MAN'S DAUGHTERS 1-5
A SAVAGE LOVE 1&2
BAE BELONGS TO ME 1&2
A HUSTLER'S DECEIT 1-3
WHAT BAD BITCHES DO 1-3
SOUL OF A MONSTER 1-3
KILL ZONE
A DOPE BOY'S QUEEN 1-3
TIL DEATH 1-3
IMMA DIE BOUT MINE 1-5
By **Aryanna**

BROOKLYN ON LOCK 1 & 2
By **Sonovia**

A DRUG KING AND HIS DIAMOND 1-3
A DOPEMAN'S RICHES
HER MAN, MINE'S TOO 1&2
CASH MONEY HO'S
THE WIFEY I USED TO BE 1&2
PRETTY GIRLS DO NASTY THINGS
By **Nicole Goosby**

THE STREETS ARE CALLING
By **Duquie Wilson**

LIPSTICK KILLAH 1-3
CRIME OF PASSION 1-3
FRIEND OR FOE 1-3
By **Mimi**

TRAPHOUSE KING 1-3
KINGPIN KILLAZ 1-3
STREET KINGS 1&2
PAID IN BLOOD 1&2
CARTEL KILLAZ 1-3
DOPE GODS 1&2
By **Hood Rich**

STEADY MOBBN' 1-3
THE STREETS STAINED MY SOUL 1-3
By **Marcellus Allen**

WHO SHOT YA 1-3
SON OF A DOPE FIEND 1-4
HEAVEN GOT A GHETTO 1&2
SKI MASK MONEY 1&2
By **Renta**

GORILLAZ IN THE BAY 1-4
TEARS OF A GANGSTA 1/&2
3X KRAZY 1&2
STRAIGHT BEAST MODE 1&2
By **DE'KARI**

TRIGGADALE 1-3
MURDA WAS THE CASE 1-3
By **Elijah R. Freeman**

MARRIED TO A BOSS 1-3
By **Destiny Skai & Chris Green**

SLAUGHTER GANG 1-3
RUTHLESS HEART 1-3
By **Willie Slaughter**

GOD BLESS THE TRAPPERS 1-3
THESE SCANDALOUS STREETS 1-3
FEAR MY GANGSTA 1-5
THESE STREETS DON'T LOVE NOBODY 1-2
BURY ME A G 1-5
A GANGSTA'S EMPIRE 1-4
THE DOPEMAN'S BODYGAURD 1&2
THE REALEST KILLAZ 1-3
THE LAST OF THE OGS 1-3
By **Tranay Adams**

KINGZ OF THE GAME 1-7
CRIME BOSS 1-4
By **Playa Ray**

FUK SHYT
By **Blakk Diamond**

DON'T F#CK WITH MY HEART 1&2
By **Linnea**

ADDICTED TO THE DRAMA 1-3
IN THE ARM OF HIS BOSS
By **Jamila**

LOYALTY AIN'T PROMISED 1&2
By **Keith Williams**

FOREVER GANGSTA 1&2
GLOCKS ON SATIN SHEETS 1&2
By **Adrian Dulan**

YAYO 1-4
A SHOOTER'S AMBITION 1&2
BRED IN THE GAME
By **S. Allen**

TRAP GOD 1-3
RICH $AVAGE 1-3
MONEY IN THE GRAVE 1-3
CARTEL MONEY
By **Martell Troublesome Bolden**

TOE TAGZ 1-4
LEVELS TO THIS SHYT 1&2
IT'S JUST ME AND YOU
By **Ah'Million**

KINGPIN DREAMS 1-3
RAN OFF ON DA PLUG
By **Paper Boi Rari**

THE STREETS MADE ME 1-3
By **Larry D. Wright**

CONFESSIONS OF A GANGSTA 1-4
CONFESSIONS OF A JACKBOY 1-3
CONFESSIONS OF A HITMAN
By **Nicholas Lock**

I'M NOTHING WITHOUT HIS LOVE
SINS OF A THUG
TO THE THUG I LOVED BEFORE
A GANGSTA SAVED XMAS
IN A HUSTLER I TRUST
By **Monet Dragun**

QUIET MONEY 1-3
THUG LIFE 1-3
EXTENDED CLIP 1&2
A GANGSTA'S PARADISE
By **Trai'Quan**

CAUGHT UP IN THE LIFE 1-3
THE STREETS NEVER LET GO 1-3
By **Robert Baptiste**

NEW TO THE GAME 1-3
MONEY, MURDER & MEMORIES 1-3
By **Malik D. Rice**

THE LIFE OF A HOOD STAR
By **Ca$h & Rashia Wilson**

THE STREETS WILL NEVER CLOSE 1-4
By **K'ajji**

LIFE OF A SAVAGE 1-4
A GANGSTA'S QUR'AN 1-4
MURDA SEASON 1-3
GANGLAND CARTEL 1-3
CHI'RAQ GANGSTAS 1-4
KILLERS ON ELM STREET 1-3
JACK BOYZ N DA BRONX 1-3
A DOPEBOY'S DREAM 1-3
JACK BOYS VS DOPE BOYS 1-3
COKE GIRLZ
COKE BOYS
SOSA GANG 1&2
BRONX SAVAGES
BODYMORE KINGPINS
BLOOD OF A GOON
By **Romell Tukes**

CREAM 2-3
THE STREETS WILL TALK
By **Yolanda Moore**

CONCRETE KILLA 1-3
VICIOUS LOYALTY 1-3
By **Kingpen**

THE ULTIMATE SACRIFICE 1-6
KHADIFI
IF YOU CROSS ME ONCE 1-5
ANGEL 1-4
IN THE BLINK OF AN EYE
By **Anthony Fields**

NIGHTMARES OF A HUSTLA 1-3
BLOOD AND GAMES 1&2
By **King Dream**

HARD AND RUTHLESS 1&2
MOB TOWN 251
THE BILLIONAIRE BENTLEYS 1-3
REAL G'S MOVE IN SILENCE
By **Von Diesel**

MOB TIES 1-7
SOUL OF A HUSTLER, HEART OF A KILLER 1-3
GORILLAZ IN THE TRENCHES
By **SayNoMore**

BODYMORE MURDERLAND 1-3
THE BIRTH OF A GANGSTER 1-4
By **Delmont Player**

FOR THE LOVE OF A BOSS 1&2
By **C. D. Blue**

KILLA KOUNTY 1-5
By **Khufu**

MOBBED UP 1-4
THE BRICK MAN 1-5
THE COCAINE PRINCESS 1-10
STEPPERS 1-3
SUPER GREMLIN 1-4
By **King Rio**

MONEY GAME 1&2
By **Smoove Dolla**

A GANGSTA'S KARMA 1-4
By **FLAME**

KING OF THE TRENCHES 1-3
By **GHOST & TRANAY ADAMS**

QUEEN OF THE ZOO 1&2
By **Black Migo**

GRIMEY WAYS 1-3
BETRAYAL OF A G
By **Ray Vinci**

XMAS WITH AN ATL SHOOTER
By **Ca$h & Destiny Skai**

KING KILLA 1&2
By **Vincent "Vitto" Holloway**

BETRAYAL OF A THUG 1&2
By **Fre$h**

RELENTLESS GOON 2 | PRINCE A. TAUHID

THE MURDER QUEENS 1-6
By **Michael Gallon**

FOR THE LOVE OF BLOOD 1-4
By **Jamel Mitchell**

HOOD CONSIGLIERE 1&2
NO TIME FOR ERROR
By **Keese**

PROTÉGÉ OF A LEGEND 1&2
LOVE IN THE TRENCHES 1&2
By **Corey Robinson**

THE PLUG'S RUTHLESS DAUGHTER 1&2
By **Tony Daniels**

BORN IN THE GRAVE 1-3
CRIME PAYS 1&2
By **Self Made Tay**

MOAN IN MY MOUTH
By **XTASY**

TORN BETWEEN A GANGSTER AND A
GENTLEMAN
By **J-BLUNT & Miss Kim**

HERE TODAY GONE TOMORROW 1&2
By **Fly Rock**

PILLOW PRINCESS
By **S. Hawkins**

SANCTIFIED AND HORNY
by **XTASY**

WOMEN LIE MEN LIE 1-4
FIFTY SHADES OF SNOW 1-3
STACK BEFORE YOU SPLURGE
GIRLS FALL LIKE DOMINOES
NAÏVE TO THE STREETS
By **ROY MILLIGAN**

LOYALTY IS EVERYTHING 1-3
CITY OF SMOKE 1&2
By **Molotti**

THE BUTTERFLY MAFIA 1-4
SALUTE MY SAVAGERY 1&2
By **Fumiya Payne**

THE LANE 1&2
By **Ken-Ken Spence**

THE PUSSY TRAP 1-5
By **Nene Capri**

DIRTY DNA
By **Blaque**

BOOKS BY LDP'S CEO, CA$H

TRUST IN NO MAN
TRUST IN NO MAN 2
TRUST IN NO MAN 3
BONDED BY BLOOD
SHORTY GOT A THUG
THUGS CRY
THUGS CRY 2
THUGS CRY 3
TRUST NO BITCH
TRUST NO BITCH 2
TRUST NO BITCH 3
TIL MY CASKET DROPS
RESTRAINING ORDER
RESTRAINING ORDER 2
IN LOVE WITH A CONVICT
LIFE OF A HOOD STAR
XMAS WITH AN ATL SHOOTER

www.ingramcontent.com/pod-product-compliance
Lightning Source LLC
Chambersburg PA
CBHW071159260626
47162CB00003B/1102